# Awakening

The Amykah Grayson Chronicles

Book One

A.G. Hughes

Printing in the United States of America

First Printing, 2024

Editor: Rachel Garber, Caroline Goldsworthy

Cover Art by Moonchildljilja

ISBN: 979-8-89316-621-7 - Paperback
ISBN: 979-8-89316-620-0 - eBook

*To Morgan - I am forever grateful for your unwavering belief in me and your constant support throughout this incredible journey.*

*To my friends and family (you know who you are) - I want to extend my deepest appreciation for your invaluable role as a sounding board and your contributions to this story.*

# CHAPTER 1

M Y HEART POUNDED IN my ears as I ran. The possibility of freedom compelled me to quicken my pace down the dimly lit hallway. I rushed past closed doors, where the other captives lay in the dark of their rooms. The smell of feces, bleach, and humanity penetrated my nostrils. My eyes darted back and forth as I tried to determine if the shapes lurking in the shadows ahead were real or just imagined. The sound of shoes pounding on the linoleum behind me threatened my one chance for escape. I glanced over my shoulder just as a massive force crashed into my tiny frame, slamming me to the ground. With one enormous hand, a musty-smelling man quickly pinned my arms behind my back while pressing my face against the sterile, cold floor with his other hand. The weight of him on my back had me gasping for air.

A beam of light appeared in the darkness, sweeping back and forth until it landed on my face.

"Amykah, calm down. We're not going to hurt you," the voice said, the words slowly rolling off her tongue.

Her steps inched closer until I found myself staring at white and paisley Dansko clogs. She leaned over with the flashlight held above her head. At this odd angle, the light made distorted shadows while her yellow toothy grin gleamed, creating an unnatural picture.

"It's going to be alright, dear. I'm here to help," she said, her brown eyes shining.

With her face inches away from mine, I could smell the mixture of coffee and cigarettes on her breath. I saw light reflecting off something shiny in her hand. She noticed me looking and hastily put her hand behind her back. She patted me on the shoulder while directing her gaze to the man on top of me.

"Hold her tightly, Stan."

Before I could protest, she jammed a large syringe into my upper arm. The liquid quickly took effect. Tension gave way to a warm rush of relaxation flooding my muscles. My body went limp, along with my hopes for escaping, as the white and paisley clogs came in and out of focus.

The man, apparently named Stan, let go of my wrists. My arms landed with a soft thud on the ground beside me. The nurse and Stan towered over me, whispering to one another. With a nod to the nurse, Stan rolled me onto my back. His thick arms scooped me up like a lifeless doll. He lumbered down the hall and the only thing I could do was stare at the ceiling and count the darkened lights we passed beneath. My eyelids grew heavier with each step he took until I could no longer fight against their weight.

When I pried my eyes open instead of darkness, blinding fluorescent lights greeted me from above. I tried to shield them and found both my wrists and ankles were bound by heavy leather cuffs while a hard rectangular object forced my mouth open.

Surrounding me were faceless beings in white coats mumbling words I couldn't understand. I turned and felt a tugging on my scalp. Wires extended from my head to a large machine with dials and switches next to my bed. Eyes wide, my pulse quickened as one of the pale-faced beings looked down on me. Its features had been melted away so only a vague outline of a mouth remained. I recoiled when its hand reached out and touched my shoulder.

"Don't worry, you will barely feel this," a man's voice said as he flipped the switch with a hint of a smile on his otherwise featureless face.

My body shook violently. I sat bolt upright, heart racing and beads of sweat dripping from my forehead. Trembling, I flung off the covers to ensure my ankles weren't strapped down. I scanned the room, trying to remember where I was. There was a nightstand with a lamp, a clock, a cell phone, and a bottle of vodka standing next to the bed. I smelled a hint of citrus and vanilla from an air freshener I spotted plugged into the wall across from me. A sigh of relief escaped my lips as the realization sunk in that I was in my apartment, far removed from the place I had revisited in my dreams.

I swung my legs out of bed and placed them firmly on the hardwood floor. The pressure of my hands on my thighs helped steady me as I took a few deep breaths. Dampness from both fear and sweat clung to my body along with the shirt I was wearing. I slowly stood, making sure my legs would support me before shuffling toward the bathroom. Along the way, I peeled off my soaking-wet shirt and dropped it on the floor.

As I reached for the light switch, an involuntary shudder ran through my body, remembering the first time electricity coursed through every part of my being during my unexpected stay at Harbor View Psychiatric Hospital.

Turning on the faucet, I let the cool water flow freely over my hands and wrists, bringing me back to the present. Splashing my face calmed the heat emanating from my cheeks. I gazed into the mirror.

The person staring back at me looked much older than she was. Purplish circles contrasted with her empty blue eyes. Dark, stringy hair hung to her shoulders and framed her petite features while emphasizing the sallowness of her complexion.

Who was this person staring back at me? I splashed a little more water on my face, searching those big blue eyes in the mirror for any recognition of the former me. The me I was before my dad died. The me I was before I lost my mind.

My first year of college should have been one of the most exciting times in my life with all the possibilities ahead of me: boys, blowout parties, pledging a sorority, but that wasn't in the cards for me.

My parents planned on me attending a college in Illinois, which meant I could come home on the weekends and spend time with the family. Although I loved the idea of being close to home and was looking forward to my mom doing my laundry, I wanted to explore other options. My sister Kate was in her final year at Northwestern, but I didn't want to follow in her footsteps. I wanted to take my own path, and thankfully, my parents humored me.

The first time I stepped onto the campus at Creighton University, it felt like home. It was an oasis nestled in a bustling downtown. Bright pink and white blossoms filled the cherry trees along the brick walkway, cutting through the center of campus. In the middle of it all sat the towering cathedral of St John's Church, where all were welcome. A man in black, sans his white collar, with rosy cheeks and a white beard, sat on a bench across from the church, waiting for anyone who wanted to chat about the meaning of life or how good the basketball team would be that year. Co-eds were scattered over the grassy knolls, reading, playing frisbee, listening to music, and laughing. A smile spread across my face. This is where I had to be. I couldn't explain it. I just knew it in my bones.

My parents were reluctant, especially my dad, to have me far away from home. I argued it was only a seven-hour drive or a quick plane ride, which really wasn't far in the grand scheme of things. Seeing all the work I had done to get scholarships and knowing once I set my mind to something, I wouldn't back down, they finally gave in.

In the end, I think it was my roommate who really sold them on the school. Lexi Strom was a native of Omaha with a fiery personality which perfectly matched her hair color. We had an instantaneous connection. She was like the sister I had always wanted, in sharp contrast to the sister I actually had. Over the summer, as we prepared for our upcoming adventure, I visited her in Omaha as often as I could, and she stayed with me in Chicago a handful of times, helping ease any remaining concerns my parents had.

That fall, I arrived at what would be my new home for the next four years with my mom and dad in tow. My dad stood out in his bright Hawaiian shirt and khakis, with his hair a little too shaggy for my mom's liking. My mom shined in her neutral pants suit, perfectly coifed hair, and sensible footwear. It always baffled me how the two of them ever entered each other's orbit, let alone got married and had kids.

We made our way to my dorm room on the eighth floor of Swanson Hall. I put my key in the lock, and the door flung open. Lexi stood in the doorway, all five-foot-ten-inches of her, flashing a grin.

"You're finally here," she said, wrapping me in a giant bear hug.

From the outside, we were polar opposites. Lexi was tall, loud, curvy in all the right places, stood out in a crowd, and could literally charm the pants off anyone. I'd actually seen it happen on one of the weekends I stayed with her during the summer. On the other hand, I was the short, girl-next-door type who felt more comfortable wearing a t-shirt and a pair of jeans, and who would rather disappear in a crowd than stand out. I was the yin to Lexi's yang.

"Come in, come in," she said.

"Hey, Lexi," my dad said, handing her a box. "Did you hear about the fire at the shoe factory?"

Taking the box and setting it on the floor, answering, "No, Mr. G, I didn't."

"Unfortunately, many soles were lost," he said, waiting for her reaction.

Lexi snickered. "That's a good one, Mr. G."

I groaned and rolled my eyes at my dad.

"I've got plenty more where that came from, Myks," he grinned. "Did I ever tell you why leopards can't play hide and seek?"

I shot him my most stern glare, as the corners of my mouth twitched with the barest hint of a smile, pleading, "Please, Dad, no more bad jokes."

"Oh, alright. I'll save them for later," he said with a wink. "Joyce, why don't you stay here and help finish unpacking while I get us checked in at the hotel? I'll grab a couple more things for Amykah at the store, then swing by here and pick you up for dinner."

Mom gave him a peck on the cheek. "Sounds good, honey."

"Lexi, would you like to join us?" he asked with a welcoming smile.

"Yeah, Mr. G, that would be great," Lexi said.

"Alright, I'll be back in about an hour or so," he said with a wave, closing the door as he left.

Immediately following his departure, Mom handed me the Clorox wipes, instructing me to wipe down every surface while she unpacked my clothes and organized my closet. My mother had this way about her: if she was busy doing something, you best get busy too; otherwise, a huge unspoken tidal wave of guilt would knock you over into begrudging compliance.

Lexi must have felt this wave because after sitting for a few minutes on the couch and getting just one sideways glance from my mother, she jumped up and started unpacking one of my boxes labeled desk.

After thoroughly cleaning every surface, I needed to wash the stink of Clorox off my hands. I opened the door to the adjoining bathroom, where I came face to face with an edgy-looking brunette showing off the double snake tattoo on her exceptionally toned arm.

"Oh, hey, sorry. I'm Amykah, and that's Lexi over there."

Her eyes scanned me up and down, and then she shook her head and shut the door.

"And that was Tori," Lexi said, placing my notebooks and pens inside the desk.

"Well, isn't she just charming? I can't wait to see more of her," I said as I rolled my eyes.

A voice growled behind the door, "I can hear you."

I covered my mouth, stifling a laugh. Lexi shot me a look, and I fell silent. Apparently, Tori was *not* someone to mess with.

Once we had completed the unpacking to my mother's satisfaction, Lexi quickly grabbed some clothes, slowly opened the bathroom door to ensure the coast was clear and dashed inside. A few minutes later, she threw open the door and strutted out.

"Really, Lex?" I raised my eyebrow. "You're going to wear *that* to dinner?"

She was head-to-toe bedazzled in sequins, jewelry, and leather.

Lexi twirled, saying, "Why, of course. Better to be over-dressed than under, I always say."

She made a face at me and gestured to my t-shirt, jeans, and tennis shoes I'd been wearing all day. "Are *you* going to wear *that?*"

"Why this old thing? It's straight off the runways of Milan," I said, doing my best to twirl around but stopping short when I saw my mother's face as she looked at her watch. I guess I hadn't really noticed the time.

"Mom, is everything alright?" I asked.

"Well, your father should have been here by now. Let me call him," she said, pulling the phone out of her purse as it started ringing. "Oh," she sighed, relieved, "this must be him. Hey, honey..."

Her smile faded quickly while the color drained from her face. In a daze, I watched her methodically place her phone back in her purse. Her face remained expressionless. She cleared her throat, then fixed her gaze on me. "Amykah, your father has been in a car accident and is at the hospital."

My throat went dry as my chest tightened. I could barely get words out.

"What? Is he okay?"

I felt a reassuring squeeze on my hand as Lexi appeared beside me.

"The nurse said he is being prepped for surgery now. She recommended we get there as quickly as possible," my mother said, hoisting her purse strap high on her shoulder.

"Can I call an Uber for you, Mrs. G?" Lexi asked with her phone at the ready.

Mom nodded. "I would appreciate it. Thank you, Lexi."

My lungs wanted to burst, but a tightness wrapped around my throat. The words wouldn't come out. I looked at my mother, trying to read her face for some clue telling me everything was going to be alright, but her steely exterior provided zero comfort. I don't know why I would think this circumstance would be any different from the previous nineteen years. Growing up, my mom was a stickler for rules, while my dad was the fun one. Of the two of them, she valued logic over feelings, always telling me how my emotions were a liability and would just get in the way.

In contrast, my dad didn't believe in black-and-white thinking. There were no rules. It all depended on the context of the situation, making everything a maybe. He exuded total acceptance no matter who or what the problem was in front of him, including me, emotions and all. I knew I wasn't going to get the support I needed from my mother, at least not in the way I wanted it.

"Hey, Mom, is it okay if Lexi comes with us?"

Lexi looked up from her phone. "I don't want to intrude."

"I think it would be good for Amykah if you were there," Mom said, half smiling at Lexi.

As we left the dorm to the awaiting Uber, the lamps lighting our path felt harsh against the soft black of the night sky. The campus was relatively empty. By the looks of it, most of the parents had already left, and the students were likely pre-gaming for the freshman welcome party starting later tonight. Lexi and I were going to join the festivities after dinner; however, it appears fate had a different plan for me. The car was waiting for us at the curb. Lexi hopped in first. I slid in next to her, and Mom followed.

"Memorial Hospital, please," Mom said to the driver, her voice one note while she stared glassy-eyed out of the window.

For the first time in my life, cracks appeared in my mother's otherwise perfect exterior. The lines on her face were somehow deeper, and her skin was a subtle shade of gray. It took a tragedy of this magnitude for her humanity to finally reach the surface.

"Mom," I said.

She raised her hand, "Not right now, Amykah. It will not do us any good to speculate. We will know more when we get to the hospital," she said with finality, her voice flat, giving no indication of what was going on inside. All my mind could do *was* speculate. Instead of giving voice to my thoughts, I kept my mouth shut. We rode in silence all the way to the hospital.

It was the longest twenty minutes of my life.

# CHAPTER 2

WE FINALLY ARRIVED AT the hospital. The crisp, cool autumn air caused chills to run up my spine. I watched my mother return from wherever her thoughts had taken her into a calm, composed woman. She smoothed out her shirt, pulled her shoulders back, lifted her head, and ran her hands through her wavy blonde hair.

She marched over to the nurses' station and spoke with authority, her face devoid of expression. "Erving Grayson, please. I'm his wife. He was in a car accident, and they are prepping him for surgery."

"I'm afraid he's already been taken to surgery. I can take you to the waiting room if you would like," the nurse replied as she rose out of her seat.

My mom held up her hand.

"That's very kind of you, but not necessary. If you could point us in the general direction, that would be enough."

The nurse obliged.

"Thank you," Mother said with a nod as we walked down the hall.

The regrettable decorating choices left the waiting room filled with more doom and gloom than comfort with its beige walls and multitude of brown chairs. Fern plants that hadn't been watered in weeks were placed strategically throughout the room, trying to brighten up the space but failing miserably. A television hung on one wall where a few people gathered mindlessly watching HGTV. Mom sat in a chair nearest the entrance, and I plopped down beside her.

"I'm going to go find us some coffee, food, or something," Lexi said, wrapping her arms around me. "Can I get you anything, Mrs. G?"

"No, thank you. I'm fine," Mom said not taking her eyes off the double doors leading to the surgical wing of the hospital.

I tried to focus on something, anything else other than what was happening. Still, my mind created images of my father lying lifeless in the car covered in blood, followed by the paramedics cutting him out of his seatbelt and placing him on the stretcher. My mind conjured picture after horrible picture of what could have happened to my dad.

I blinked in rapid succession and found Lexi standing before me, her arms loaded with chocolate bars, candy, and assorted chips.

"Want anything?" she asked with a half-smile promptly dropping the contents of her arms on a table.

I shook my head as tears streamed down my cheeks.

A nurse wearing a surgical gown came through the door. Mom looked up and the nurse motioned her over. She stood and quickly covered the distance between them meeting the nurse in the doorway of the waiting room.

"Mrs. Grayson, can you and your daughters please come with me?" she said in a low voice.

"Oh, no, I'm just a friend of the family," Lexi corrected her while pulling me to my feet. She placed a welcoming arm around my shoulder and walked me over to my mother. "I'm here if you need me," she said, squeezing my arm before flopping down in the nearest chair and grabbing a bag of chips.

I took my mother's hand in mine as we followed the nurse down the hall. Even if she didn't need the support, I did. The nurse opened the door to a small, windowless room with three grey chairs, a tiny steel table, and a box of tissues. They seriously needed to find a new decorator.

"What is going on?" my mother questioned.

The nurse swallowed deliberately, avoiding eye contact with either of us.

"The doctor asked that I come out and give you an update," she said, her voice shaky.

"Why would we need an update? Didn't he just go into surgery?" my mother asked.

"Well, yes. However, things aren't going as planned. We ran into some unexpected complications and are not sure he is going to make it," the nurse said, looking at me and then back to my mother. "I have to go now. The doctor will be in shortly. I am so sorry."

She exited the room, closing the door with a soft click.

"This can't be happening," I said, wrapping my arms around myself, rocking back and forth. Pressure was building inside my chest, and I felt lightheaded. I needed to do something. I got up and started pacing the small room like a caged animal.

"What did she mean by, 'we are not sure he's going to make it'? It doesn't make any sense. Dad is healthy and strong, so why would..."

"Amykah, stop. Honey, please, stop," Mother said in a quiet voice while she stared at the floor with her head in her hands.

The creak of the door opening had us both up on our feet. The doctor walked in and immediately shifted his gaze to the floor. He lowered himself slowly into a chair, wringing his hands. Finally, he broke the silence by clearing his throat and looked at my mother.

"Umm, I don't know how to say this Mrs. Grayson, but your husband didn't make it."

My mother swayed, grabbing onto the wall to steady herself. I doubled over, clutching my stomach as if the doctor had gut-punched me. I couldn't breathe. The knot in the pit of my stomach made its way up to my throat, choking my cries.

"What happened?" my mother whispered.

"I honestly have no idea. Everything was going well, and then his heart stopped...he was just gone. I tried everything I could to bring him back, but nothing worked."

Even the doctor looked stunned by the turn of events.

"I am truly sorry for your loss," he said, patting my mother's hand. He paused momentarily, looking at my mother and then at me. He nodded and walked out the door.

The pressure was crushing my lungs, and I couldn't hold it in any longer. The lump in my throat gave way to sobs. I crumpled to the ground.

My mother was next to me, pulling me in tight to her. The warmth of her arms and the steady in and out of her breath were comforting. But the pain grew in my chest, becoming so sharp I thought for sure my heart was breaking.

There was a gentle tap followed by the door clicking open.

"Um, excuse me. I'm sorry to interrupt, but I need to review some paperwork with you, Mrs. Grayson. Would that be okay?" the nurse asked.

I peered through the puffiness surrounding my eyes and looked at my mom. Her eyes were rimmed red, and her cheeks stained with tears. She just nodded a silent yes. Then she got up and left with the nurse, leaving me alone.

I reached for the box of tissues on the table. A pain throbbed in my head. My heart felt like it was being squeezed by a vice as the realization my dad was gone hit me. I was never going to see him again wearing his silly Hawaiian shirts, never hug him again, never be able to ask him how to fix something again, and never hear him make his stupid dad jokes again.

My breath caught as the click of the door sounded, and my mother walked in.

"Okay, Amykah. It's time for us to go," she said, her voice thick, reaching her hand toward me.

"What do you mean to go? How can we leave Dad here?"

She sat down next to me on the floor and brushed the hair out of my eyes like she did when I was little.

"Amykah, your dad is not here anymore. His body may be, but the dad we knew and loved is gone."

My body shook with sobs. All I could do was hang my head and nod. She helped me up off the ground. When I stood up, the room swirled around me, causing me to lose my balance. I couldn't get my bearings and fell back into a chair, closing my eyes.

"Are you alright, honey? Amykah?" my mother asked, but her voice sounded a million miles away.

I tried opening my eyes again, but the room still spun around me as the floor fell from under my feet. My stomach churned. A light touch brushed my shoulder.

"I'm going to go get the nurse," Mom said as she left the room.

Finally, the spinning came to a stop. Fluttering my eyes open, the room came into focus and was back to being solid. However, I couldn't say the same for my stomach. With a click, the door opened, and my mother entered first, followed by the nurse.

I blinked rapidly in disbelief. Every muscle in my body went on high alert as my heart raced. A triangular head sat atop a long neck with bulbous green compound orbs looking me up and down. I rubbed my eyes, trying to make the vision disappear, but it didn't. It was as if the nurse was superimposed on top of the creature. When the creature moved, the nurse moved. When the creature talked, the nurse spoke. All I could hear was someone screaming. Then I realized it was me.

It moved toward me, slowly reaching out a triple-jointed spiky claw cloaked as the nurse's arm. I swatted it away, climbing on the chair, ready for a fight.

"Don't touch me," I yelled, grabbing my phone from my pocket and hurling it toward its head.

My mother's face blanched, and her mouth went slack, but she wasn't looking at It; she was looking at *me*. Shielding Its mouth, the creature whispered something I couldn't hear. My mother nodded, and It left the room.

"What the hell was that thing? We have to get out of here," I said, jumping off the chair and grabbing my mom's arm. I started pulling her toward the door, but she stood unmoved.

"Amykah, we can't leave yet."

"What do you mean we can't leave yet? Didn't you see that thing? It wasn't human. It was wearing the nurse like a costume. We have to get out of here." I tugged her arm even harder.

A familiar click and the door opened. It came in, and It had friends. In an instant, I was thrust onto the ground while some*thing* held onto my arms, and another held my legs. My face smashed against the threadbare carpet. I could see my mother out of the corner of my eye, hands on her mouth, tears rolling down her cheeks. She was just standing there, watching, doing nothing to help me.

"Let me go!" I thrashed, trying to break free of their grip.

I felt a sharp sting in my arm and turned my attention to where it came from. I was eye-to-eye with It. A singular black spot in a sea of green focused on me while its antennae twitched back and forth. It smiled, bringing the vice-like ridged jaws together.

"It's going to be alright, dear," It clicked.

A warm sensation flooded my body.

"Get away from..." I tried to finish the sentence, but my speech slurred nonsensically. My body was sluggish and unresponsive to my thoughts. The last thing I saw was my mother standing beside the creature, looking at me. Hoping this was all just a bad dream, I closed my eyes and let the sedative coursing through my veins pull me into the darkness.

# CHAPTER 3

A S THE MEMORY OF that fateful night faded, I stared at my reflection. An empty shell of a girl stared back. I once was someone who had endless possibilities at my fingertips and my whole life in front of me, but all that was gone in an instant. I felt like I'd been through a lifetime in just one short year.

After my father's sudden death and what was deemed an acute psychotic breakdown, I spent six months at Harbor View Psychiatric Hospital trying to make the demons go away. That was the only word I had at the time to describe the horrific creatures that stalked me in the dark of the night. Once I was regarded as stable, I was released to the care of my mother, who acted as my guardian until I could prove I was a functioning member of society. Thankfully, it was a short-lived situation, two months to be exact. I think both of us were secretly relieved when she was released as my guardian and could return to her life in Chicago.

And now, here I was, standing in the bathroom of my own tiny one-bedroom apartment, just a few minutes from Creighton, the campus I hoped to attend once again in Spring. I went to my weekly therapy sessions and held down a job for the past four months at my neighborhood Trader Joe's. All of those accomplishments meant I was back on the path I had set out for myself. Then why couldn't I shake this feeling of dread that something terrible was just around the next corner? I always seemed to be holding my breath, waiting for the other shoe to drop.

Just then, I caught a glimpse of two glowing red spots reflecting in the mirror from my room. I glanced over my shoulder, but there was nothing there. I must have imagined it. I took one more look at my reflection and switched the light off.

I grabbed the first dry shirt off the floor and slipped it on before falling into bed. The clock on my nightstand read 2:11 a.m. Thankfully, it was Friday, and my next shift at the grocery store wasn't until Sunday.

The half-full bottle of vodka called out to me, promising to lull me to sleep. The familiar room-temperature sting felt good in the back of my throat. I took a few more drinks, thanking my sleep aid. The warmth of relaxation filled my body and mind as I cozied up under the blankets. I rolled over on my side, closing my eyes with a sigh. A subtle chill rose up my spine, causing the hairs on the back of my neck to strain away from the skin.

The feeling of some*one* or some*thing* standing next to my bed, watching me, gripped my mind with fear. Adrenaline coursed through my veins. Every muscle in my body ached, ready to escape.

I had experienced this feeling before in the psychiatric facility. Most of the time, nothing was there when I opened my eyes. But, on a few occasions, I wasn't alone, and my screaming rapidly brought attention to the situation only I could see. I was given a cocktail of clear liquids in a syringe and would drift off into a dreamless sleep.

Right now, I wish I had that option, but it was just me in my apartment, and no old night nurse with a yellow smile was coming to save me. I couldn't just lay here all night, paralyzed by fear. I took a controlled breath and counted to myself: one, two, three. My eyes flew open. Nothing. There was nothing there. I let out a sigh of relief and rolled onto my back. My mouth went dry as a little squeak escaped my lips. Hovering over me, close enough to touch me but showing no indication of doing such a thing, were two glowing red eyes shrouded by a hood.

I sprung into action and flung myself onto the floor on the opposite side of my bed. Pressing my body against the hardwood, I scrunched my neck to get a better view. My eyes settled on the bottom of a black cloak hovering just above the floor. Heart pounding, I squeezed my eyes shut tightly. *It's just a hallucination, nothing more. It's not real.* I kept repeating those words in my head over and over until the sense of something being in the room gradually faded. I slowly opened my eyes. The cloak was gone. I crept up the side of my bed and peered over the edge. Whatever it was, it was gone. I slumped against my bed, head in my hands. The air I'd been holding in the whole time finally escaped.

I picked myself off the floor and stomped to the bathroom. I glared at the girl in the mirror. I hated being like this, not in control of my own mind. Unsure of what was real and what wasn't. Flinging open the medicine cabinet, I grabbed one of the prescription bottles and threw the lid on the ground. A few pills landed in my hand, and I slung them into the back of my throat, swallowing hard. I slammed the medicine cabinet shut. The mirror cracked, and what I saw was a shattered version of myself looking back at me.

Making my way back to bed, I grabbed my phone from the nightstand, opened my contact list, and pressed call. I knew the office wouldn't be open, but I could at least leave a message. It rang and rang, finally a click with the standardized message followed by a beep.

"Um, yeah. This is Amykah Grayson. I need an emergency appointment today with Dr. Blythe. Just tell him the visions are back, and he'll understand. Um, thanks. Bye."

I returned my phone to the nightstand. The vodka bottle was bathed in a pool of light. Taking it as a sign from above, if I believed in that sort of thing anymore, I pressed the open bottle to my lips and drained every last ounce of the welcome nectar into my body. Although not recommended, I hoped the combination of medication and vodka would knock me unconscious. So even if something returned to watch me sleep, I wouldn't notice, let alone care.

The loud ring from my phone jolted me out of my stupor. My head, heavy with a deep ache, was a good indication I had slept the rest of the night. I wiped the drool from my mouth and reached for the phone, accidentally knocking over the empty vodka bottle.

"Ummm, hello?" I said, my throat thick with inflammation.

"Is this Miss Grayson?" the voice on the other end asked.

Rubbing my eyes, they adjusted to the light of the morning sun pushing its way through my closed blinds.

"Yeah, it is. Can I help you?"

"Hello, Miss Grayson. This is Nicole from Dr. Blythe's office. He said he could squeeze you in at ten a.m. Does that work for you?"

"Yeah, sure. I'll be there. Oh, and thank you."

"You're welcome, Miss Grayson. See you soon."

I looked at my phone and then glanced at the clock on my bedside to confirm the time.

"Oh, crap! It's already 9:15."

I attempted to jump out of bed, but the sheets had wrapped around my legs in my sleep. My body hit the floor hard. I untangled my legs and scrambled to my feet, sprinting around the room for some clothes. Black bra, black t-shirt, and black jeans, my standard chosen uniform. I sniffed the shirt. The scent of vanilla with just a hint of stench hit my nose. It would have to do, and I slipped it over my head. I pulled on my jeans and found my steel-toed boots by the bedroom door.

I dashed to the bathroom for a quick once-over. Puffy red eyes stared back at me. Ugh. I opened my medicine cabinet and popped in a couple of eye drops. Then, attempting to multitask, I tried to tame my bedhead with one hand while simultaneously brushing my teeth with the other. When I finished, I looked at my distorted reflection in the cracked mirror. An old nursery rhyme started playing in my head.

*All the king's horses and all the king's men*
*couldn't put Humpty together again.*

I grabbed my black hoodie and bag. "Hopefully, Dr. Blythe can put you back together, Humpty," I said to the warped girl looking back at me.

As I made my way through the living room toward the door, I skidded to a halt. There was an envelope lying on the floor.

It had my name scrawled on it. I shivered at the thought of someone sliding this mysterious envelope under my door in the dark of night. I'm not sure how long I stood there and stared at it before finally gathering enough courage to pick it up. I took a deep breath and slid my finger under the edge of the envelope. Inside was a small folded-up piece of paper. I took it out and read the words written in the same scrawled handwriting:

*You've been asleep for too long.*
*If you don't want to end up like your father,*
*you must wake up and see the truth. See you soon.*
*~ C*

# CHAPTER 4

*I*'VE BEEN ASLEEP FOR *too long?* Whoever left me this note doesn't know me very well because I barely sleep at all. And as for ending up like my father, what the hell does that even mean? My father died on the operating room table after a car accident. Why would I end up like him? Unless...maybe whoever left this note was insinuating it wasn't an accident after all? No, that's impossible. I read the note a few more times, flipping it over in my hands. Someone is just messing with me. But who and why now? I jumped when the alarm went off on my phone, sending the note flying into the air. I watched as it floated to the ground. I'd have to deal with it later. Right now, I needed to catch the bus.

I rushed out of my apartment, slamming the door behind me. The clomping of my boots echoed in the empty stairwell. My mind raced, and my feet ran toward the front door. Stepping outside into the bright morning sun, a searing pain ran through my head, a not-so-gentle reminder of the amount of vodka I had drank last night. I shaded my eyes from the glare as the bus stop came into focus.

The bench was occupied by an older woman tending to her knitting and two teenagers who were clearly playing hooky from school. Standing beside them was a gorgeous man with dreadlocks falling to his waist, oversized pants, sneakers, and a puffy blue jacket, listening to his headphones. Then there was Joe. Each day, Joe sat in his well-worn spot near the bus stop, holding his 'Will work for Food' sign. I nodded as I passed by him, just as the bus squealed to a halt.

I waited for my fellow riders to board the bus. Once inside, I greeted the driver while glancing around for a seat. The teens had made their way to the back of the bus, where a few of their friends were waiting. The beautiful man managed to capture the only seat at the front. I passed by a mother putting her young daughter's hair into pigtails. There was an empty seat halfway back. The older woman, who had been sitting on the bench earlier, looked up from her knitting. Her bright eyes crinkled when she smiled at me, revealing a partially toothless grin.

I slid next to the window and put my bag on the open chair next to me as a deterrent against potential company. Joe caught my eye as I stared out the window, trying to comprehend what I saw. His gaze was intent on me.

He raised his sign up so I could see; it now read:

*Nothing Is As It Seems*

I looked at the sign and then back at Joe. Our eyes met. He pointed to the sign, and although I couldn't hear him, his lips relayed the message. *Nothing is as it seems.* I squeezed my eyes shut for a split second and opened them to find Joe sitting on the ground, holding his cup out to receive generosity from a passerby. His sign leaned against the bus stop and read, 'Will work for Food.'

Unease settled into my bones. What was happening to me? The last time I had these kinds of delusions, I was in Harbor View. I shuddered and pushed down the memories clawing at the back of my mind. The most likely scenario is I've developed a tolerance to my current medication. Dr. Blythe said it could happen. That's all this is—a simple change to my medication, and everything will go back to the way it was.

My mind drifted back to the note left at my apartment.

*You've been asleep for too long.*
*If you don't want to end up like your father,*
*you must wake up and see the truth. See you soon.*
*~C*

I racked my brain trying to think who would be cruel enough to play that kind of sick joke on me, and only one person whose name started with the letter C popped into my head, Cassandra. She was in the mental institution at the same time I was there. I have no idea what I had done to her, but she made it her mission to make my life a living hell. Is it possible she got out, found me, and decided to continue what she started?

"You think you can hide? We know who you *really* are," a voice whispered in my ear.

I whipped my head around and glared at the man sitting directly behind me. He was staring out the window, listening to something on his headphones, completely oblivious to what was happening. I turned around and focused on the stained seat in front of me, trying to ignore the taunting voices.

"Just look. Everyone is staring at you. They know who you are, just like we do. You can't hide anymore," the voice insisted.

A shiver crept up my spine as an eerie calm blanketed the inside of the bus. I slowly raised my gaze and was met by black eyes staring back at me everywhere I looked. Even the sweet little girl with pigtails holding the teddy bear bore a hole into my soul. All the color had been swallowed up. Even the whites were gone.

They all slowly tilted their heads in unison, keeping their unblinking eyes fixated on me. I tried to scream, but I couldn't catch my breath. My vision tunneled and stars flashed before my eyes. On the verge of passing out, I cradled my head in my hands, closed my eyes, and waited for the feeling to pass. The eerie calm faded while the activity on the bus whirled back to life. The vice grip on my throat started loosening, allowing air to enter my desperate lungs. I took a few shallow breaths, feeling the burn of bile rise in the back of my throat.

I slowly peeled my hands away from my eyes. Everything was as it should be. The mother was now putting a pink bow in her daughter's hair, the older woman was knitting, and the teenagers were at the back of the bus doing what teenagers do.

I shifted in my seat and slumped down as low as I could. I don't understand how the hallucinations have gotten so bad so quickly. I was startled back to reality by the vibrating coming from my bag. I pulled out my phone. Heaving out a sigh, I touched the red cancel button. I don't know why my sister would be calling me. We haven't talked in months. Today, of all days, I just couldn't handle another passive-aggressive conversation with her blaming me for everything that's ever gone wrong in her life since our father's death. I dropped my phone back in my bag, and glimpsed a little clear bottle with a blue label peeking out from under my wallet. I had forgotten I had put it in there as the day's first smile crossed my lips.

I wrapped my whole hand around the little bottle and pulled it out of my bag. Turning my body to hide my illegal activity,

I heard the subtle crack as the lid twisted off in my hands. I slid lower into my seat. My dry throat welcomed the liquid. I swallowed in succession until the little bottle was empty. The warming sensation enveloped my body, and my thoughts drifted to happier times.

"Next stop, Twelfth and Main," a booming voice said from above.

I jumped to my feet before the bus stopped, squeezing by the people patiently waiting to exit the bus with a polite 'excuse me'. The bus driver opened the doors and in my rush to get out, I missed the last step and crashed into a giant Paul Bunyan of a man.

"Open your eyes. It's time you woke up to the truth," he said, his eyes fixed on mine.

"I'm sorry, but what did you say?" I said, holding onto his arm and staring at him in disbelief.

"I said you should open your eyes and watch where you're going," he said, pushing me back upright while removing my hand from his arm. I watched him trudge onto the bus and sit by the window, not returning my gaze.

I turned away as the bus left and walked toward the twelve-story brick building. The next thing I knew, I was in the lobby without even opening the door. That's when I spotted a handsome young man wearing a crisp business suit. He had a briefcase in one hand and was still holding the door open with the other. I cocked my head to the side as I looked in his direction.

"You're welcome," he said, locking his grey eyes onto mine.

He felt familiar somehow, which seemed ridiculous because I'd never met him before this moment. I shook my head, chalking it up to my mind playing tricks on me, not having enough sleep and being hungover.

"Umm, thank you," I said with a half-hearted wave.

He smiled, a dimple showing up on his right cheek.

"Now, was that so hard?" he said, giving me a wink while the door slowly closed behind him.

# CHAPTER 5

I STUMBLED ACROSS THE lobby and found myself in front of the elevator bank. A man wearing a pair of shiny black shoes topped with black slacks stood beside me. The elevator opened with a ding. A black mist rolled out along the floor while people exited the elevator, completely unaware. It seemed to have a life of its own. I shuffled my feet backward so as not to let it touch me. The mist approached the shiny black shoes and slowly swirled up around the man beside me, wrapping him in darkness. When it reached his face, the black mist pulled back, creating a space as if taking a breath. Then, it suddenly pierced his eyes and penetrated his nose and mouth, disappearing into him completely. The man swayed, then regained his composure. He turned to me, his eyes black as his shoes.

"After you, miss," he said, drawing out his words and gesturing to the elevator.

"Um, no thanks, I'll catch the next one," I said, the words rushing out.

The man shrugged, entering the elevator, saying, "Suit yourself."

I glanced at him one last time before the doors started closing. His eyes had returned to a normal hazel color. He caught me looking at him, and the black of his pupil spread out, devouring all the color while an unnatural smile spread across his face. I held my arms tightly to my body to stop myself from visibly shaking.

When the second elevator arrived, a rush of people came out. I darted inside and pushed the button for the twelfth floor. Finally alone, I exhaled. The hallucinations were becoming severe and frankly terrifying, but not as terrifying as the thought that I might be headed back to Harbor View.

Arriving on the twelfth floor, I stepped out into an empty hallway. Dr. Blythe's office was the first door on the left. My hand trembled, reaching for the doorknob. I quickly shook it out, took a deep breath, and opened the door.

The office was sage, white, and brown, with cozy chairs lining the walls. Tasteful abstract artwork was peppered around the room, with green succulents nestled quietly in each corner. A little side table boasted coffees and teas, inviting you to relax while you waited. As I approached the front desk, I walked by a few other patients sitting in chairs, keeping themselves busy.

"Good morning," the receptionist said, looking up from her screen with a smile.

I leaned forward on the desk, speaking in a hushed tone, "Um, I'm here to see Dr. Blythe for my ten o'clock."

"Have a seat, Miss Grayson, and we'll call you back shortly."

She smiled politely and turned her attention back to the computer.

I sat beside the fish tank and watched the yellow and orange fish hypnotically swim back and forth. The familiar buzzing of my phone let me know I had a message waiting. There was no number attached to the cryptic message that read:

*There are unseen lions all
around you waiting to pounce,
stop being a sheep and
open your eyes to the truth
or you'll end up like your father,
dead.*

Just then, Dr. Blythe, a big, burly man in his mid-fifties, wearing a suit with a button barely holding him together, appeared at the door. He motioned for me to join him. My balance teetered as I made my way back to his office. He ushered me to a couch that had seen better days while he sat in an overstuffed chair across from me. A large plant, two bookshelves overflowing with books, and a lamp gave the room an overall warmth.

"I got the weirdest text, Dr. Blythe," I said as I handed him my phone. "Something about lions all around and stop being a sheep, or I will end up dead like my father? It just popped up on my phone with no number attached. I also got a similar message shoved under my door this morning. Weird, right?"

He examined the screen and handed the phone back to me.

"Is that what you saw?" he asked, eyebrows raised.

"Yes...Wait, what did you see?"

He reached for a pen and notepad off his desk.

"Nothing, there was no text."

"But it was just there, I swear. I'm not making it up," I said, frantically scrolling through my texts, trying to find what I saw. But just like he said, it wasn't there. I stared at my phone and shook my head.

"Amykah, I got your message from this morning. Can you tell me what happened?" he said.

I sighed.

"Well, as you know, the nightmares started a couple of weeks ago, which I didn't really think was a big deal. It wasn't until last night that I had a full-blown hallucination and then this morning, they have continued to intensify."

"Tell me exactly what happened," he said, his pen at the ready.

I rubbed my forehead, recounting the details of the morning. A deep crease formed between his eyebrows. He looked up from the notepad.

"It is odd the hallucinations have returned so abruptly and all at once. Amykah, do you remember what today is?" he said slowly.

"Umm, Friday?" I asked.

He smiled.

"Yes, it is Friday. But it is the date I am referring to, a significant date for you."

He paused, looking for my reaction.

I shrugged.

"It's the anniversary of your father's death and the day you were admitted into Harbor View," he said, keeping his eyes on me.

My heart sank. I hadn't realized it was *that* day, or maybe I just didn't want to.

"What does that have to do with my hallucinations coming back?" I asked.

"Well, in the few months you have been coming to see me, you have avoided addressing your emotions surrounding those two events. What you went through, Amykah, was traumatic on many levels, and that kind of trauma doesn't stay suppressed. It has a way of bubbling back up to the surface and coming out in ways you least expect, despite your best efforts. I suspect the traumas of that day and the six months you were in Harbor View are breaking through into your conscious mind, resulting in hallucinations."

He sat awaiting my response. I didn't know how to respond. Instead, I got up and walked over to the window to stare at the bustling city below. Dr. Blythe remained silent, patiently waiting. It was too much for me to bare.

"So, you really think the reason the hallucinations are coming back is because I'm not dealing with..." I bit my lip unable to finish.

"It is a definite possibility," he said.

"All I want is to get back to my normal life, the life I was supposed to have before everything happened. I'm really trying, Dr. Blythe. I've submitted my application to go back to school next year. I've held a job and been a solid employee." My voice cracked as the tears broke through and flowed down my cheeks. "I just want to be the girl I used to be, the carefree one who only had to worry about her grades, hanging out with her friends, and which party to go to."

"Now, Amykah," he said, his voice softening, "you know that's not how it works. You can't go back; you can only move forward, integrating the new pieces of you instead of hating them."

I faced him, the tears still streaming.

"But I don't know how to do that. How can I accept what shattered me into a million pieces and stole away my future?"

Dr. Blythe's chair creaked as he leaned back into it, eyes fixed intently on me. I sat back on the couch and promptly examined the back of my hands. He let out a heavy sigh and glanced at the clock.

"Ok, Amykah. Here's what we are going to do. I'm going to increase your dose of Haldol and prescribe a medication to help you sleep. I will call these into your pharmacy so you can pick them up immediately. I want you to come in twice a week so we can monitor your reaction to the medication and make adjustments as needed. We will also be working through the grief of losing who you were, your previous life, and how to embrace the person you are now. No more avoiding."

I nodded, standing to shake his hand.

"Thank you, Dr. Blythe."

He took my hand and patted me on the shoulder, ushering me to the door. A sense of foreboding engulfed me as I entered the empty hallway. I pushed the feeling down, telling myself it was nothing. Because for the first time today, I felt hopeful, and I wasn't going to let anything take it away from me.

# CHAPTER 6

I BREATHED IN THE cool, crisp air and exhaled a sigh of relief as I exited the building. Making my way to the pharmacy, a quick five-block walk, I kept my head down and put one foot in front of the other. As I continued to walk, questions swirled around my head, begging to be answered. Who sent the note? Was it even real? Would the meds actually work? Was I just buying time to avoid the inevitable...being sent back to Harbor View? Before I knew it, I arrived at my destination.

The automatic doors opened. I made a beeline to the back of the store, maintaining my focus on the ground while simultaneously bobbing and weaving through other customers until I reached the pharmacy counter. I raised my gaze to see a statuesque Amazonian Barbie woman with long, flowing raven hair and a perfectly proportioned frame talking on the phone. She made eye contact with me and pointed to the chairs behind me. I took a seat and busied myself with my phone, waiting to be summoned to the counter when it was my turn.

"Excuse me, Miss, how can I help you?" A man's voice said, cutting like a knife through the noise surrounding us.

I lifted my head and found my eyes resting on perhaps the most stunning man I had ever seen standing where the Amazonian Barbie once stood. I walked over to the counter in a daze. I was looking at a paradox. The angles of his face were chiseled yet soft. He was tall and thin, yet I could see his toned arms and pecs through his tight white button-down shirt. His eyes were icy grey with a twinkle, nothing like I had ever seen. But something niggled in my mind. I had seen those eyes before, but when and where?

I felt a gentle pressure on my wrist.

"Miss, are you okay?" he asked.

I blinked slowly, forcing myself into the moment, and saw his hand placed tenderly on top of my wrist. A pulsating heat caused my skin to tingle under his touch. My cheeks flushed. I don't know how much time had passed as I stood there just staring at him. I quickly pulled my hand from his and looked away.

"Um, yes. Um, I'm here to pick up a prescription."

"Name?" he asked as a smile spread across his beautiful mouth.

His voice was silky smooth and unruffled. His eyes waited for mine to meet them once again. No matter how much I didn't want to, I had to look. I was transfixed.

"Amykah. Amykah Grayson," I choked out.

"Ah, yes, Miss Grayson. Let me get that for you," he said, disappearing into the stacks of medication.

Flopping back into the chair I had been sitting in earlier, I put my head in my hands. My cheeks still carried the heat from our interaction. I picked up the magazine sitting on the makeshift table next to my chair and thumbed through it. My mouth fell open when I saw the title of an article.

*The World You Live In Is A Lie. You Need To
Wake Up To The Truth.*

"Miss Grayson, your prescription is ready."

I jumped up, startled by my name. He raised an eyebrow, fighting the urge to smile. My legs felt weak, and another heat wave raced to my cheeks. I looked back at the magazine I had thrown on my chair and saw the rest of the title.

*How to tell if your boyfriend is cheating on you.*

I shook my head at the lengths my mind would go to create messages for me that weren't there.

"Here you go," he said, placing the bag on the counter.

He smiled, and if teeth could sparkle, his would have. I grabbed the prescriptions and shoved them into my bag. Our eyes met briefly, and he gave me a wink that sent electricity up my spine.

I hurried toward the exit without even a thank you, leaving behind the grey-eyed mystery man and my complete and utter humiliation. As soon as I cleared the automatic doors, I reached into my bag, grasping for my salvation, only to find it wasn't there. It had to be. I know I put it there. I plopped on the sidewalk and promptly poured out the contents of my bag onto the ground. As I sorted through it, a man handed me a dollar bill.

"Oh, no. I don't..." I protested, but he was already gone.

I could see why he thought I might need help, what with all my belongings spread on the sidewalk outside a pharmacy. I put everything back into my bag one by one. The prescriptions were not there. I slung my bag over my shoulder and stood up. Making my way back through the sliding glass doors, I trudged to the pharmacy counter once again. There stood the Amazonian Barbie with her beauty pageant smile.

"Thank you for your patience. I had to attend to an urgent matter. How can I help you?"

Her magnificence overwhelmed me, and all I could do was stare.

"Are only beautiful people allowed to work here?" I asked half-jokingly.

"Pardon?" she said with her head tilted to the side.

"Um, sorry. The other pharmacy assistant helped me while you were gone."

She furrowed her brows.

"What other pharmacy assistant?"

"Um, he's about six foot tall, with short, spiky blondish hair and grey eyes. I didn't get his name, though. Anyway, he gave me my prescriptions. Well, at least I thought he had. When I left, I couldn't find them in my bag. So, he must have taken them back or something."

I clamped my mouth shut to stop myself from blathering on and on.

She shook her head, and her long, flowing raven locks followed suit.

"Oh, I am so sorry for the inconvenience. What was your name again, Miss?"

"Grayson. Amykah Grayson."

"Oh, that's odd. Your prescriptions are sitting right here."

She picked up the package next to the register and handed it to me. This time, I watched my hand carefully deposit the medications inside my bag. Then, I double-checked to make sure it was still in there.

"Well, that was easy," she said. "I'm still not sure who helped you, though. Anywho, I am sorry for the inconvenience."

I put my hands down on the counter and stretched up on my toes, trying to see if I could spot him.

"Could he have come in to relieve someone and then left?"

She followed my gaze and then looked back at me with her brows furrowed and lips pursed.

"There is only one man working today. Let me go get him and see if we can solve this mystery," she said with a nod.

I watched her walk away and disappear into the back. She returned, escorting a short, stalky man with sweat beading on his forehead. He looked at me through his thick black eyelashes.

"Is this him?" she asked with a hopeful smile.

"Um, no. That is definitely *not* him," I said, shaking my head.

"Ok, thanks, Jim," she said, waving him off as he dashed back into the depths of the office.

I wasn't going to let it go that easily. I knew he had to be there somewhere.

"Well, what about a store employee? Could they have popped back there and helped me when you were away?" I asked, looking around the store.

"I'm sorry, Miss, there is no one who works in this pharmacy or in this store fitting the description you gave," she said while she glanced at her computer and raised an eyebrow.

Wrinkling her nose, she mumbled, "Hmmm."

"What?" I said as I cocked my head to look at her.

"Oh, it's nothing," she said with another wave of her hand. "Is there anything else I can help you with? Do you need any instruction regarding your medications?"

Her voice had a hint of condescension. Then, it dawned on me what was happening. She had looked at the computer and saw the medication I was on.

"Wait a minute, do you think I made him up?" I whispered, looking around to make sure no one could hear me.

She flushed, then quickly spun around.

"Oh yes, Jim, I'll be right there," she yelled toward the office, clearly making any excuse to get out of explaining what she was insinuating about me. "I'm needed in the back. If there is nothing else I can help you with..." She turned and left, with the end of the sentence and her accusation hanging in midair between us.

I hurried out of the store, avoiding eye contact with other customers on my way out. A fire burned through me as I went through the automatic doors to the fresh air outside. She thought I had actually made him up, that he was a figment of my imagination. I kept replaying the scene in my mind while I paced back and forth on the sidewalk. He was there. I felt him touch my wrist. He handed me my prescription...but did he really?

I stopped pacing. Self-doubt infiltrated my mind, dissolving the anger into insecurity. It wasn't in my bag when I left the first time. Could I have made him up? Could it all have been a hallucination? My head began to hurt. I rifled through my bag and found my prescriptions. Fighting against the tiny staple refusing to let me get to my medication, I ripped off the top and grabbed the Haldol. The lid came off the bottle with one quick twist. I sent the pill to the back of my throat and swallowed hard, hoping it would return me back to some semblance of normality.

# CHAPTER 7

I WAS GREETED BY a brown paper package sitting on the welcome mat outside my apartment door. My name and address were spelled out in big block letters, with no indication of where this mysterious package could be from. It was an awkward size and heavier than I anticipated. Trying to hold the package while opening my door proved challenging, and the package landed on the floor with a thud.

I grabbed a knife from my kitchen and slid it carefully through the heavily taped edges. As the brown paper wrapping fell to the floor, another package was revealed with a note taped on top of it.

*Dear Miss Grayson,*

*It has been brought to my attention that a package bequeathed to you by your father was recently discovered. Unfortunately, due to a clerical error and lengthy time in probate, the package was sent to the Unclaimed Property Division. While work-ing on a completely unrelated case, my paralegal stumbled upon your package and made me aware of the matter. Please accept my sincerest apologies for the delay. Contact me if you have any further questions.*

*Regards,*
*Harry P. Jensen, J.D.*
*Jensen & Jensen Law*

My hands shook as I took out a book wrapped in silk and tied with a linen string. An envelope was carefully tucked under the crisscrossed cords with my name written in my dad's handwriting. My breath caught in my throat. I slowly slid the envelope free and pulled out the note inside. My eyes brimmed with tears while I read my dad's words.

*My Dearest Amykah,*

*I am sorry to have left you. There is so much I wish I would have told you sooner, but I wanted you to remain safe and grow up having a life free from the darkness. I knew you had the sight when you were young, which I slowly watched become dor-*

*mant as the veil between ego and soul descended. You were so young and happy as a child. I didn't want to burden you with the weight of our lineage and its role in the fight for humanity.*

*I left you unprepared for what I am sure you started experiencing at my death. This world is not what it seems. There is a plane that coexists with ours. One filled with Darkness and creatures only seen in nightmares. Our family has been fighting for generations to save humanity from being overtaken by the Dark. I have left you the one thing that can help you as you awaken to the truth of who you really are: this book. It is the culmination of my years hunting and killing the Darkness.*

*Our lineage has been passed down through my side of the family. I learned everything from my mother, your grandmother, and she learned everything from her father, your great-grandfather, and so on. It was evident to me you had the gift and a destiny, but I was never sure of your sister. She had always been so logical, believing only what could be determined by the senses, never showing any indication of the unseen world. Keep an eye on her rld. Keep an eye on her though, she may yet still awaken and need your guidance. As for your wonderful mother, whom I loved dearly, she had no knowledge of the separate life I led, and I wanted to keep it that way.*

*I know you must have a million questions, my dear, and I'm sorry I can't be there to answer them and guide you through what is to come. There are Institutes for those like us, and once you awaken, you will be found. We Awakened often have a way of finding one another. Keep yourself safe and alive until then.*

*Love, Dad*

My mouth went dry as I stared at the note. Another plane coexisting with ours? Maybe my dad had delusions and hallucinations, too. I'd never considered my sudden psychotic breakdown might be inherited. But if that were the case, wouldn't I have heard something about my father or grandmother having a breakdown at one time or another? They both had mentally and physically demanding jobs requiring them to travel all over the world and interact with a number of people. I don't think they could have hidden a mental illness without *anyone* finding out. It just doesn't make sense. There had to be another explanation.

I pulled the twine, and the silk cloth fell away, revealing a rough leather-bound journal. It was wrapped with a thin strap, keeping the thick, heavy pages safely hidden. I unwound the strap and flipped through the pages.

There were hand-drawn pictures of creatures I had never seen before, one more terrifying than the other, with names and detailed descriptions scribbled in my dad's handwriting. My hand stopped on one called The Cogere. The picture staring back at me was a creature hunched on all fours with a large muscular back where two wings were drawn. Horns protruded from its head while sharp talons looked as if they were gripping the page.

I turned the page, wondering what I would find next. My heart skipped a beat, and tightness gripped my chest. At the top of the paper was written the word Kuzatuvchi. Right below it was drawn a cloaked figure with two red eyes. It was the creature in my room this morning. What are the odds both my dad and I had hallucinated the exact same creature? I continued reading. *I caught this creature standing over Amykah one night. I discovered, through means I will not disclose, it was known as the watcher, sent by the Dark to watch over Amykah and report back if she was a threat.*

Forgotten memories flooded in from my childhood. I remembered that night. I woke up screaming. My dad came running in and fought with the creature, subduing it. He knelt by my bedside, placing his fingers on my temples. His voice was calm and hypnotic, telling me it was all just a bad dream and to go back to sleep.

I started recounting all the times Dad had gone on a trip for work and came home with a great story to tell about how he'd broken his arm, got a black eye, or had cuts and bruises from a fall on the dig site. One time, when I was eight, I stumbled across a hidden compartment in the back of my dad's office closet while playing hide and seek with my sister, Kate. He walked in and caught my arm just as I was about to touch one of the blades. When I asked what they were, he explained he was a collector of medieval weapons and they were hidden for safekeeping.

I shook my head. How could I have forgotten all of that? The buzzing of the intercom startled me out of my memories and back to reality. Tucking the note from my dad inside the book and quickly wrapping it closed, I shoved it under my couch. As I walked toward the door, my mind conjured up creative excuses, eager to get rid of whoever was there. The intercom crackled to life with a press of a button.

"Hello?"

Silence.

"Hello? Is anyone there?" I asked.

A heavy pounding on the door filled the air. I peered through the tiny door lens and saw a green eye looking back at me. I closed my eyes, inhaled deeply, and exhaled with a big sigh. I needed to figure out what the package from my dad meant and if it was even real, but I couldn't do that right now. Right now, I had to open my door and see what my friend had in store for me.

As soon as the door lock clicked open, a rush of glorious long red hair tickled my face, the smell of pepperoni and cheese pizza saturated my nose, and a large duffle bag smashed my shoulder.

Lexi Strom was the only friend who stood by me this past year. She visited me every week at Harbor View for the entire six months I was there. After, when I stayed with my mom, she would come over for movie and game nights. Lexi never treated me any differently than the first day we met. I am forever grateful for her friendship, even if her showing up today couldn't have come at a worse time.

She put the pizza on the coffee table and spun around. Her face was ear to ear with a devilish grin. Grabbing a tie off her wrist, she swept her bangs out of her eyes while placing her fiery hair into a messy ponytail. Lexi was dressed in jeans slung low on her hips with holes everywhere and a cut-off t-shirt of some band from the 80s.

"What's all this?" I asked.

"I thought you needed a fun girls' night out," Lexi said with a smile.

"Oh, Lex, I don't really feel up to a night out. I didn't sleep well last night. Can't we do it some other time?" I said, glancing toward the book, making sure it was safely hidden from view.

Lexi raised her eyebrows with a devious twinkle in her eye.

"Oh, no. I've got plans for us tonight. You can sleep the rest of the weekend. Come on, Myks, it's going to be fun."

I sat down and grabbed a slice of pizza, trying to come up with a solution I could tolerate.

"How about we go to the Mai Tai Lounge? I think that's all I can handle tonight."

Located under a motel, a dimly lit stairwell with shag carpeting on the walls led you down to the secret entrance of the Mai Tai Lounge. The solid entry gave no indication of what lie on the other side. Prying open the heavily weighted door revealed a floor-to-ceiling red Tiki bar. Red carpet, red chairs, and red-painted ceiling tiles. They had decorated each wall differently. Wood paneling covered one, another with gold lamé, and yet another with shag carpeting, all adorned with velvet pictures of naked women.

"Nope. We are going to Club Inferno," she smirked.

I grunted as I threw myself into the cushions, my head landing on the back of the couch with a thud.

"Really, Club Inferno? And who is this 'we' you are talking about? Don't they card everyone at the door and..." I asked, biting into my pizza.

Lexi reached into her bag and flashed two IDs.

"Don't be such a downer. Tori is meeting us there," Lexi said.

I let out an audible sigh.

"Tori? The girl with the double snake tattoo I lived next door to for a day in the dorms. That Tori?"

Lexi looked at me, her brows knitted together.

"I know she didn't leave a good impression the first time we met her, but I've gotten to know her pretty well this past year, and we've become friends. She's usually up for anything I suggest, no matter how crazy. Not to mention, she's a real badass when it comes to fighting. Can you at least give her a chance?" she said, tossing me one of the IDs. It came flying at me like a ninja throwing star. I ducked as it hit the back of the couch.

"A trick I learned, courtesy of Tori," Lexi said with a bow.

"I suppose...but how much does she know about what happened to me?" I asked, taking another bite of pizza, trying to look unconcerned.

"She only knows your dad died suddenly, and you took a year off to deal with it. I didn't tell her anything else. That's your story to tell, not mine," she said.

I picked up the ID that had fallen. It had my picture and name; the only difference was the year I was born, making me twenty-two instead of nineteen. My mouth dropped.

"Lexi, where did you get these? They look real," I said, turning it over.

"I got a guy," she said with a shrug as a mischievous smile crossed her lips. "Ready for a night of depravity, Miss Grayson?" she said, the heavy black eyeliner highlighting her green eyes.

"Do I really have a choice?" I asked.

She just shook her head, her eyes gleaming in anticipation like a kid at Christmas.

Lexi brushed, tugged, and decorated me while I patiently waited for the reveal. Then she threw some clothes at me.

"Here, put these on," she said with a nod.

Dear God, what have I gotten myself into now? I stood with my back to the full-length mirror, prepared to see the result of Lexi's makeover. She spun me around.

"Ta-da!" She said, arms spread wide, her face beaming.

My mouth fell open as I looked at my reflection. Black leather pants hugged my non-existent curves like they had been painted on. A black skin-tight leather tank top clung to my abdomen like Saran Wrap. The tank, combined with the push-up bra Lexi had brought for me, made my waist look tiny and magically created cleavage. The only thing that felt like me was my black steel-toed boots I'd chosen to wear despite Lexi's protests.

She had slicked my dark hair back into a smooth ponytail, putting my face on display. I wasn't a fan of letting the world see me, let alone my face. However, she did some kind of witchcraft because the dark circles were gone, and my blue eyes were piercing as they stared back at me. Even I thought I looked sort of pretty.

"Lex, I don't know about this," I said, shaking my head.

She grabbed me from behind and rested her chin on my shoulder.

"You look amazing! Why not try being someone other than yourself for just one night?" She kissed my cheek and patted my ass. "Now it's my turn," she said, grabbing her bag and slamming the bathroom door behind her.

Here was my chance. I rushed out to the living room and reached under the couch for the book, but my hand couldn't find it. Dropping to my hands and knees, I stretched my arm all the way under the couch, searching for the book, but came up empty. I got up and looked around. The box the book came in was sitting on the floor. Where was the note from the lawyer? I searched the box, picked it up, looked under it, and went through all my papers on the table. It wasn't there. What the hell was going on? I turned my entire living room upside down, looking for any evidence the box's contents existed, but found none.

"Amykah, I'm ready to make my entrance," Lexi yelled through the bathroom door.

I sprinted into the bedroom just in time.

My jaw dropped when Lexi opened the door. She raised her arms overhead as her bangles fell, hitting each other while swiveling her hips to the music they made. Lexi's choice of outfit for the evening was a barely there mini skirt with a complimentary bustier the color of the ocean and black fishnet stockings. Red hair was piled atop her head in a loose chignon with tendrils strategically placed to frame her face.

"That was the response I was hoping for," she said with a Cheshire cat grin.

She grabbed her purse and made her way to the door.

I looked one more time at my reflection and let out a sigh. I don't know if I am losing my mind or if someone is trying to prevent me from learning the truth. Then Lexi's words rolled around in my head *'Try being someone else tonight'*. "I would love to be somebody else tonight," I said to the beautiful stranger reflected back to me.

# CHAPTER 8

I STARED OUT THE window as we drove down Dodge Street, passing by Goldberg's familiar red awning on the left, then Midtown Crossing with its beautifully designed park and shops on the right, and finally reaching the Gene-Leahy Mall at the Riverfront. Our driver turned into the Old Market district, taking us to our final destination. When we arrived at the club, I took in what my night beheld and let out a sigh.

Lexi reached over me to open the Uber door and promptly started shoving me out of it, saying, "Come on, Myks, this is going to be fun."

"I very much doubt that," I said, resisting her push as much as possible, which proved difficult for my five-foot-three-inch frame.

We stood outside the ominous, all-black building just as flames burst forth from the walls, illuminating the sign *Club Inferno*.

"Do I *have* to go in there?" I asked.

Ignoring my pleas, she took my hand and skipped us to the front of the line. I could hear a collective groan behind us with a few choice words shouted in our direction. Lexi was never one for waiting in lines or following the rules, for that matter.

"Back of the line, miss," the bouncer said gruffly, keeping his eyes plastered to his clipboard.

Lexi sauntered over to him. "Hello, sir." She batted her eyelashes and smiled. "My, your shirt can barely contain you. Looks like your pants are having a difficult time as well."

I swallowed hard, which sent me into a coughing fit. Lexi looked at me, asking silently if I was okay. I nodded, and she turned her attention back to the bouncer. She always seemed to know exactly what to say and when to say it. Unlike me, she never cared about what other people thought of her. It's one of Lexi's many superpowers I wished I had.

The flames glistened off his smooth head. A subtle flush crept into his chiseled cheeks as his gaze met Lexi's. She slowly traced her finger down the bouncer's arm from his shoulder to his hand, holding the clipboard and artfully arched her back so he could view her braless cleavage.

"We are on the list. See, right there."

She pointed randomly at a name while biting her lip, not taking her eyes off the bouncer.

The bouncer's gaze never wavered away from Lexi. She slid her hand up his arm, resting it on his shoulder, and leaned in, whispering something in his ear. A smile slowly spread across his gruff exterior. Then she gave his ear a little lick. I shook my head. Lexi's charms had snared yet another. There was no question we were getting in now. He stood holding open the velvet rope as another collective groan rose from the crowd.

"Thanks, you're a doll," Lexi said, grabbing his ass.

"So much for needing our IDs," I whispered into her ear.

She gave a little shrug. "Don't worry. I guarantee they will come in handy for us in the near future."

As we entered the club, my senses were assaulted. The pungent smell of sweat pouring off bodies writhing all over each other on the dance floor wafted in from the adjacent room. Men and women wearing costumes that left very little to the imagination gyrated in cages that hung from the ceiling. The general stickiness of everything all around us was palpable. A tap on my shoulder jolted me out of my own personal hell that was *Club Inferno*.

Lexi pointed toward the back room, where the loud music poured out, and shadows of writhing bodies lurked. I shook my head, bringing a pretend cup to my mouth. To get through this night, I would need a drink.

She yelled, "There's a bar in the back," and pulled me, against my better judgment, toward the shadows.

The oppressive heat enveloped me like a wet blanket as we approached the metal gates that gave entrance to the back room. Beads of sweat formed at the back of my neck, threatening to make their way down between my shoulder blades. We went through the spiked iron gates to what felt like Dante's 2nd circle of hell. Thankfully, Lexi guided me toward the bar at the far wall, away from the pit of sexual desires.

That's when I saw her leaning against the bar, with the unmistakable double snake tattoo on her toned arm, sipping on what looked like a whiskey neat. Tori could have been a character straight out of an action movie with her army green cut-off tank highlighting her six-pack abs, camo pants, flawless features, and a tight braid extending down her back.

Lexi made a beeline toward her and promptly gave her a big hug. Tori stood motionless as she quickly patted Lexi on the back and exited the embrace. She was clearly not someone who enjoyed hugs, but tolerated it from Lexi.

"I'm so glad you could meet us, Tor," Lexi beamed.

"Me too," Tori said, with a wry smile while she downed her drink.

"Hey Tori," I said, giving a half-hearted wave.

She nodded in my direction, looking less than enthused to have me there.

Lexi leaned with her back against the bar, lustfully looking at the dance floor potentials. The bartender, a handsome, tall man with a tank top showing off his muscular physique and black pants that fit in all the right places, leaned on the bar close to me while staring at Lexi's chest.

"Excuse me, could we get some drinks?" I shouted, but either he didn't hear me or completely ignored me. Then Lexi's words from earlier rang through my head again. *Try being someone else.* I snapped my fingers before his face, breaking him free from the Lexi spell.

He cheerfully yelled, "What can I get you?"

"A whiskey neat," Tori said as she pounded her empty glass on the bar in front of him.

I leaned in to ensure he could hear me, "A vodka soda."

He touched Lexi on the shoulder.

"And you?"

She spun around, one eyebrow raised, her tongue tracing the outline of her lips, "I'll have the same as what she is having," tilting her head toward me.

The bartender could've burst into flames from the heat pouring out of Lexi's eyes. He stood for a moment, his mouth open, unsure of what to do next.

"Drinks, go get us some drinks," Tori barked, shooing him away.

He promptly closed his mouth, turned around, and disappeared behind the bar. I sat down on the nearest stool while Lexi continued to peruse the dance floor with her gaze.

Upon his return, he informed us loudly, "This first round is on me, ladies," clearly directing his advances at Lexi in hopes of some fulfillment of them during the evening.

Lexi gave him a nod and a wink, then motioned for me to go onto the dance floor.

"Oh, *hell* no! I need a *lot* more of these before I go out there."

She turned to Tori and held out her hand. Tori just picked up her drink and took a sip. Lexi shrugged and made her way to the floor. She enchanted every handsome man she passed by touching them along the way. I sat and watched. Soon enough, she was surrounded by sweat, smiles, and bulging body parts, all hoping to win her full attention.

To say hanging out with Tori was uncomfortable was an understatement. The last time we met was a year ago in the shared bathroom of our dorm. I opened my mouth and closed it a few times before finally speaking.

"So, Tori, what are you studying in school?"

She looked at me with a blank expression, then promptly cracked her neck.

"I'm going to see if I can find some trouble. I'll be back in a bit."

And with that, she grabbed her drink and promptly left as the sea of people magically parted to let her through. My gaze drifted toward the iron staircase winding to only what I could assume was the VIP section. I looked from one face to another, making up stories about each person I saw and why they would be there. Standing at the edge of the railing was a well-dressed young man with a solid yet soft jawline, who caught my eye. And I couldn't be sure, but it looked like his icy grey eyes were staring back at me. He smiled and winked. My heart skipped a beat.

I gasped and quickly looked away. Staring intensely into my vodka soda, I tried to catch my breath. The glass met my lips, and I promptly drained the liquid like my life depended on it. With my heart pounding, I glanced over my shoulder to discover he was gone.

"Can I get you a refill?" I spun around and was greeted with a smile from the bartender.

"Sure. I'd appreciate it."

He sat a freshly made drink in front of me.

"I thought you might say that," he said with a grin.

I grabbed the drink and took a gulp. Out of nowhere, the eerie calm I'd experienced earlier on the bus descended. Slowly, everyone in the club came to a stop, and time was frozen. I cautiously looked around to discover I was the only one witnessing this strange occurrence.

Out of the corner of my eye, I saw something on all fours stalking across the dance floor, its talons scraping against the concrete, sending chills up my spine. It came to a sudden stop. Its brown leather hide stretched taut against the muscles underneath while bony ridges protruded where a spine would be. The beast rose on its hind legs, towering over Lexi. A high-pitched shriek swelled in its throat, piercing my ear drums.It stretched out one of its talons toward Lexi's neck.

"Lexi!" I screamed involuntarily. My hand released the glass I was holding, and it fell toward the ground unnaturally in slow motion.

The beast whipped its horned head around, bearing its fangs. Its black eyes fixated on me. A low guttural growl escaped from its jaws vibrating my body.

The crash of the glass finally hitting the floor broke the spell. I looked down at the shattered remnants. When I looked up, everything was as before: music playing, lights flashing, people dancing, with no creature in sight.

I felt pressure on my shoulder from behind. Every muscle in my body tensed. I slowly turned around to see the well-proportioned bartender with a concerned look. His mouth was moving, but I couldn't make out his words.

"Are you okay?" he asked, yelling over the music and gesturing to ensure I understood.

I swayed as I stood up, but not from the alcohol. My hands gripped the bar stool so I wouldn't fall. Forcing a laugh and a smile, I waved him off, doing my best to stay composed.

"No, I'm fine. I just need to splash a little water on my face."

I turned from the bar and strode toward the iron gates. His gaze felt heavy on me as I walked away. Once I reached the threshold to the front room, I looked over my shoulder. The bartender had already zeroed in on another beautiful woman at the bar. With his attention diverted, I dropped the facade and pushed through the crowd, knocking over whoever I needed to in order to get to the women's bathroom.

I bolted through the door into an empty restroom. The light from the wall sconces cast a red glow over everything. Standing in front of the mirror, my reflection stared back in disbelief.

I turned on the faucet and let the cool water run over my hands. My breath returned to normal, and the trembling slowly faded away. I pressed my wet hands against my forehead and cheeks, trying to cool the heat emanating from them. The drops of water slid off my face one at a time, causing a soft plunk when they landed in the sink. The cold porcelain against my palms felt reassuring. I took a deep breath and sighed. Out of nowhere, a tingling sensation raced through my body, causing goosebumps to form on my arm as the hairs on my neck stood at attention. My stomach felt hollow as all the sound was squeezed out of the room. A hot, moist breath tickled the back of my neck. I lifted my head slowly, seeing its reflection in the mirror.

The familiar low guttural growl escaped through its sharp, razor-like teeth, with its black eyes staring me down. I wanted to scream and run, but instead, I stood motionless. Something inside me told me not to move or look directly into its eyes. I lowered my gaze first and then my head while slowly reaching to turn the water off. Squeezing my eyes closed as tightly as possible, I waited for what would come.

Just then, a loud group of drunk women burst into the bathroom. Startled, my eyes flew open. Staring back at me was only my reflection. I examined my hands, which were completely drained of blood from the death grip I'd had on the sink.

A short brunette with freckles matching the color of her eyes looked at me. Her speech was slurred, but not so much I couldn't understand her.

"You okay?" she said as her eyes tried to focus on me.

I nodded and forced a smile.

She patted me on the shoulder and stumbled her way into a stall.

Checking my reflection, I was white as a ghost. I pinched my cheeks, adding some color to them. The vision of the beast filled my head with its talons, horns, wings, and razor-sharp teeth. It was the beast I saw in my dad's book, well at least I thought I had. My mind was betraying me. I wasn't sure what was real anymore.

I returned to the spot where Lexi had been dancing with a beautiful guy who could have been mistaken for a Greek god, but she wasn't there.

"Where did my friend go?" I asked, grabbing the Greek god by his shoulders.

He shrugged, turning to dance with the next closest woman in his vicinity.

I scanned every direction and couldn't find Lexi, but I spotted Tori standing at the bar. I pushed my way off the dance floor to get to her.

"Have you seen Lexi? I can't find her."

"No, not since I left you. I wasn't able to find any trouble either. This place is boring," Tori said putting down her drink, clearly irritated with the lack of excitement.

I pulled my phone out of my pocket. It was almost midnight. I called Lexi's phone, which went straight to voicemail.

"Amykah, what's wrong with you? You look terrible," Tori said.

What was I supposed to tell her? That I was losing touch with reality because I saw a beast almost slice Lexi's throat and then follow me into the bathroom? That didn't seem like a very good plan.

"Look, I'm worried something may have happened to Lexi. I can't see her anywhere," I said.

"She is probably here somewhere, in a dark corner, doing things that are likely illegal in three states," Tori mused. "Let's have a quick look around before jumping at shadows. Okay?"

"Fine," I said with a huff.

I scanned the dance floor, looking for her fiery red locks, to no avail. Tori had taken off to check out the other areas of the club. My eyes scoured the faces of every person on the VIP balcony and the stairs leading up to it, but no Lexi. I headed toward the tables tucked away in the darkness directly underneath the staircase, and that's when I saw him. I couldn't move. I could barely breathe. Piercing through me like a knife were those otherworldly eyes from earlier at the pharmacy standing against the wall.

A firm pressure gripped my shoulder. I spun around quickly to find Tori staring at me. I finally exhaled.

"Did you find Lexi?" she asked.

"No," I glanced back toward the wall, but he was gone. My shoulders slumped as I looked at Tori. "You?"

She shook her head.

"Maybe she went home or home with someone," Tori suggested.

"Lexi wouldn't leave without telling me first. Let's check the front room and then outside," I said.

Tori nodded.

We made our way to the front of the club as the music from the other room faded into the distance. I still hadn't spotted her yet. Something was bothering me, and I couldn't quite put my finger on it. Just disappearing was so uncharacteristic of Lexi, especially when she said this night would be a girls' night. She would never just bail on me and leave me at a club alone with Tori.

I attempted to squeeze by the other club goers who were trying to get in, but it was useless. It wasn't until Tori stepped in front of me that every person got out of the way, creating an unobstructed path leading out of the club. I stopped to look around, hoping to spot Lexi somewhere outside. The hairs on my neck prickled as a high-pitched ringing penetrated my ears. I saw Tori in front of me talking, but I couldn't hear what she was saying. Out of the corner of my eye, I saw a shadow slink across the underside of the awning.

The creature moved with cat-like stealth each leg bent at the knee in an unnatural way while its thin scorpion tail hung down, whipping from side to side. It sniffed the air, slowly turning its head 180 degrees to look at me. My body stiffened as our eyes met. I was expecting to see the face of an animal, but instead, black stringy hair fell away from the pale, grotesque, twisted face of a human. It bared its sharpened teeth and hissed at me, then started advancing across the ceiling in my direction, keeping its black eyes intent on me.

I shoved Tori into the street without a thought as to on-coming traffic, needing to get us both to safety and out from underneath the awning.

"What the hell, Amykah?" Tori said, shoving me away.

She stomped across the street to the sidewalk opposite from whatever that thing was.

I ran after her while almost getting clipped by oncoming traffic. Tori turned to confront me, but instead, her eyes focused on the club, and her body tensed. Her hands balled up into fists. Could she see it? I didn't look back, but its hiss echoed in my ears.

"Tori, do you see something?" I asked, hopeful I wasn't hallucinating, but at the same time terrified that it would mean the creatures were real.

She shook her head and shrugged. "I thought I might have seen Lexi, but it wasn't her."

My heart sank. So then she didn't see the creature, which means I'm still delusional. I jumped at the tapping of a spindly finger on my shoulder. My heart skipped a beat. I whirled around to see an abnormally tall, pale, thin man whose face, limbs, and fingers appeared disproportionately longer than the rest of his body. He was wearing a black top hat on his large head. He looked human enough, but I had to be sure he wasn't just another hallucination. I looked at Tori to see if she was also seeing this odd man.

Tori widened her stance and crossed her arms. She tilted her head down ever so slightly and stared right at him.

"Excuse me, are you Amykah?" he said with a deep rasp.

Tori and I exchanged looks.

"And who exactly wants to know?" Tori said, puffing her chest out, ready to start the fight she couldn't seem to find earlier.

The tall man slowly shifted his gaze away from me and turned toward Tori. He cocked his head, examining her closely, and blinked. When he blinked, I swore I saw a third whitish inner eyelid cross over his eye. A crooked smile spread across his lips as he stared at her.

"They said you had the sight," he said, turning his attention back to me and taking a step closer.

As he approached, I stumbled backward. Tori caught my arm just in time to stop my fall. I regained my balance while she maintained a firm grip on my arm.

"Who are you anyway, and how do you know my name?" I asked.

The tall man, whose cadence when speaking was abnormally slow and drawn out, put a spindly finger on his mouth and started tapping his lips, looking into the distance. He appeared to be pondering what and how much he should tell us.

He lowered his gaze back to meet my own.

"I saw your friend," he said.

"What friend?" I asked.

There was a long pause as the man gathered the saliva in his mouth with his tongue and swallowed. Tori tapped her foot.

"Get on with it old man," she snapped.

I could see the muscles in his jaw tighten underneath his taut, almost translucent skin. He cleared his throat and continued.

"The one with the fiery red hair."

"Lexi?" I asked, my eyes widening.

"Hmmm, is that her name? Yes. That one," he said.

"What else do you have to say, old man?" Tori growled, moving her hands to her hips and shifting her weight back and forth between her feet, looking like she was ready to fight.

He raised an eyebrow.

"You know, I don't have to tell you anything. I could just let your little friend rot," he waved his skeleton-like hand in the air.

Tori stepped toward him with her hands drawn into fists. The odd man towering over us tilted his head, the corners of his lips twitching.

"I don't think you want to do that," he said, waving his finger at Tori.

"You have no idea what I want to do right now," she challenged.

He stretched up to his full height, towering over her. "I know who you are, and if you don't want me to spill the beans, I suggest you back off, little girl."

Tori's eyes went wide, clearly taken off guard by what the odd man said. Her jaw clenched. I could tell she was about to do something stupid.

I stepped in between them. "If you know where Lexi is, please tell me."

"She has been taken," he said, softening his stance.

"Taken? Where? By Who?" I asked.

His eyes slowly scanned the area around us.

"They took her into a warehouse over on 10th street. I think I saw an H&B logo on the front of it," he said.

"We should call the police."

I extracted my phone from my pocket.

"I wouldn't do that if I were you," the man said, taking his long finger and pushing my phone down. "They won't consider her missing until the twenty-four-hour mark has passed, and by then, who knows what condition she would be in?" he said as his lips curled ever so slightly.

"But if she has been kidnapped, then surely they would..."

His eyes danced while a smirk spread across his face. "Would what? Do you actually think they would listen to two girls who have clearly been drinking in a club they got into illegally using altered official government documents?"

I shoved my phone back into my pocket.

"Well, what do you suggest we do?"

"Maybe you should go look for her," he said, eyeing Tori pick up a broken glass bottle off the sidewalk.

In one swift move, she had the bottle at his throat.

"How do we know you didn't take her?" she growled.

"Enough!" his voice boomed.

The bottle crashed to the ground. Tori's face went white. I turned my attention to the odd man, and in that moment, I saw his true face, one with no skin, no muscle, only bones with hollow, empty eye sockets staring back at me. I recoiled and screamed, making everyone around us stop and stare.

The odd man noticed the crowd. He closed his eyes, took a long, deep breath, and straightened his shirt with his long, tapered fingers. I spun around to find Tori shaken. I had never seen her like that. Her tough exterior shattered.

"You need to go and find her right now before anything done to her cannot be undone. I have said all that I came to say and now I shall take my leave" he said, turning his back on us and disappearing into the night.

"Do you think he was telling the truth? Doesn't this seem crazy? I mean, who would want to kidnap Lex? Maybe she did go home with some guy and just didn't..."

"Do you always talk this much when you are freaking out?" Tori asked, her tough exterior solidly back in place. "Here's what we are going to do; we will go to the warehouse to see if Lexi is, in fact, there. If she isn't, we will call the police and report a missing person."

"And if she is?" I asked.

"We'll get her and bring her home with us," Tori said matter of fact.

"How are we going to do that? We don't know how many kidnappers there could be. Shouldn't we call the police if we find her there and let them take care of it?"

"Fine," Tori said, rolling her eyes. "If we find her there, we will call the police. I never get to have any fun."

The streets of the Old Market became more desolate and dark the farther away we went from the club and the closer we got to the old warehouse district. Tori plucked a wayward metal pipe sticking out of a dumpster we passed by.

"What's that for?" I asked.

"You never know when you might need to defend yourself," she said as she masterfully whipped the metal pipe around her body and then over her head.

"How do you know how to do that?" I asked, eyes wide.

"I've learned a thing or two," she said without explanation.

Unsure of why I would even be interested or what prompted the question, I asked, "Do you think you could teach me?"

She stopped, looked me up and down, and shrugged.

"I guess anything is possible," she said as she walked down the street whistling.

A feeling of unease settled in my stomach. I would have sworn I was stuck in a dream, more like a nightmare of my own making. It all felt so real – the hallucinations, the envelope shoved under my door, the note and mysterious package from my dad disappearing, the demons at the club, and Tori, who seemed unfazed that we were about to break into a warehouse to save my best friend who had supposedly been kidnapped. Since I apparently can't trust my mind, I will have to put my faith in Tori, for now anyway.

I ran to catch up with her.

"Ow, what was that for?" she said, rubbing the spot on her arm I had pinched.

"Just checking to make sure you were real," I said with a forced smile.

She rolled her eyes as we continued to walk side by side into the darkness.

# CHAPTER 9

A LARGE WAREHOUSE WITH the H&B logo loomed directly in front of us. A gentle hum filled the air while a light flickered above the door to the right of the loading bay. There wasn't another person in sight, just a few random cats rummaging through the garbage; at least, that's what I was telling myself they were.

As we approached the entrance, I asked, "What do you think the chances are the door is unlocked?"

Optimistic the door was open and we wouldn't be adding forced entry to the trespassing, I reached out, placed my hand on the door handle, turned, and pushed. My heart sank.

"Um, zero to none, by the looks of it," Tori said, peering around the side of the building and then disappearing. "Amykah, come here. I think I found our way in."

As I rounded the corner of the building, Tori was pointing at something. I followed where her finger directed and saw a fire escape leading to the warehouse's second floor.

We walked over to the fire escape, and both looked up. The ladder was safely tucked away from people like us who would try to break in. I glanced around and spotted a large dumpster on wheels.

"Hey, do you think that could work?" I said, pointing to the dumpster.

"That's not a stupid idea," Tori said surprised.

"Thanks, I think," I said, unsure if she was complimenting me or insulting me.

I started walking over to the dumpster with Tori in tow. We got to the back of it and pushed. Surprisingly, it was easier to move than I thought it would be. We pushed it right under the ladder. Tori squatted against the dumpster so I could use her thighs to leverage myself onto the top of it. Thankfully, the leather pants were very forgiving and flexible. Then Tori leapt onto the top of the dumpster like it was nothing, landing in a crouch without so much as a sound. I stared at her in awe.

"How did you do that?" I asked, realizing she was very physically skilled for someone who was only nineteen.

"Gymnastics since I was five," she said, reaching for the ladder. "You go first."

I climbed up the ladder to a landing and then another flight of stairs to the top. Tori followed, arriving shortly after me. That's where we found a window, our only hope of entering the warehouse.

"Fingers crossed, it's not locked," I said as Tori stood watch. I slid my hand along the edge of the window, grabbed at whatever little ledge I could, and pulled it toward me. It opened.

Tori grabbed the window and held it above our heads.

Thankfully, solid ground was not too far down from the window's ledge. I let go of my grip and landed with a thud. As soon as I got my balance, I prepared to help Tori in the window to find she had already landed next to me with feline grace. My eyes widened in disbelief.

"That can't all just be from gymnastics training," I said.

Tori shrugged, dusting her hands and clothes off. It took a few seconds for my eyes to adjust to the darkness of the warehouse. The moonlight streamed through the dirty windows, casting shadows that danced on the concrete floor below.

The warehouse was empty, sans the inches of dust and the occasional rat scurrying across the floor. Straight ahead of us was a metal staircase leading to the main floor below. Glancing over the railing, my eyes could make out two things: the front door we unsuccessfully tried getting in and another door with a soft light coming through frosted glass at the very back of the main room.

"I'm betting that's where we need to go," I said, pointing to the door below.

I followed Tori down the staircase. The clomping of my boots on the metal echoed through the warehouse. She turned and glared at me. From that moment on, I painstakingly lowered my foot onto each subsequent step without making a sound. Once we were on the main floor, we heard a muffled thud followed by the window slamming shut above us. I grabbed Tori by the arm and quickly pulled her under the stairs.

"Didn't you close the window?" she grumbled, seemingly unruffled by the potential threat of being discovered.

"I think so, but maybe it didn't close all the way?" I whispered.

I looked toward the second-level landing and the staircase we had just descended. I couldn't see anything. I started to move, but Tori grabbed my hand and pulled me back under the stairs, shaking her head. Realizing she had left the metal pipe outside by the dumpster, Tori looked around for some kind of weapon. She settled on an old dusty mop propped against the cement and deftly separated the handle from the head. She pointed at me and then the floor, indicating I should stay put. Then she pointed two fingers at her eyes and then up at the second level, which I guess meant she would check things out.

Tori slowly inched out from under the stairs, mop handle at the ready, scanning the room. I heard nothing and saw nothing. I watched Tori strategically check the warehouse as if it were something she did all the time. There was definitely more to her than met the eye. Tori motioned for me to come out from under the stairs.

"We're okay. There's nobody else here," she said in a hushed tone.

I came out from my hiding place and walked with her toward the frosted glass door. "If we find anything, we will call the police immediately, right Tori?" I asked, wanting to ensure she was on board with my plan. Just as I turned to look at her, she dropped to her knees, her eyes wide, with one hand grasping her throat and the other one holding the mop handle.

I tried asking her what was wrong but had difficulty catching my own breath. There was a pressure all around me, squeezing the air out of my lungs. I couldn't breathe. My body was no longer under my control, and I fell to my knees, gasping. I saw Tori collapse to the floor out of the corner of my eye. She wasn't moving.

The door was about twenty feet in front of me, and if I could just reach it, we would be okay. I tried crawling, but my muscles gave way. The next thing I felt was the cold concrete against my face. My vision blurred as my eyelids grew heavy. Then, a shadowy figure appeared over me. I tried to speak but could only gasp. I lifted my hand just off the ground. Instead of taking my hand, it rolled me onto my back. The darkness had all but eclipsed my vision when I saw the shadow at my feet. A firm pressure gripped my ankles and began to drag me toward the door while my arms followed lifelessly behind. My lungs screamed for air that wouldn't come. There was no fight left in me. All I could do was let go and let the shadow take me.

# CHAPTER 10

MY EYES FLEW OPEN to nothing but darkness. I filled my lungs with a much-needed breath. Was I dreaming? A sharp pain pounded through my head. I went to rub my forehead but was stopped short. I soon discovered why. A large metal cuff enclosed my wrist. There was a chain passing through another small loop attached to a second metal cuff on my other wrist. I followed the chain with my fingers and discovered two more identical cuffs bound my ankles. This was definitely not a dream.

My breath quickened as my lips and fingers began to tingle. I needed to calm myself down if I had any chance of getting myself out of this predicament. Instead of doing what I wanted to do, which was to completely freak out, I inhaled through my nose and slowly exhaled through pursed lips to a count of ten. I repeated this a few times until the tingling disappeared. Then, I focused on my surroundings to see if I could find any clue as to where I was and how to escape. I closed my eyes. There was a subtle rhythmic swaying in my body, like I was on a moving vehicle of some kind. I ran my hand against the floor and was greeted by a smooth surface while the smell of pine mixed with dirt and sweat permeated my senses. My head grazed the ceiling, and my back was pressed against a wall. I tried to extend my legs in vain as my toes ran firmly into another wall.

The momentary sense of calmness I felt slipped away when the realization I was chained inside a wooden crate on a boat or maybe a truck taking me to an unknown destination. I kicked at the wall with my steel-toed boots over and over. When that didn't work, I wedged my feet against the opposite wall and pushed back, hoping the wall behind me would give way, but it didn't. I pulled against the chains, imitating some actor in a movie I'd seen recently trying to create enough friction or force to break myself free. Apparently, that only works in Hollywood.

"Amykah."

My body froze as I held my breath. Did I just hear a man say my name?

"Amykah, I need you to listen to me," the voice continued.

I pulled at the chains and kicked my feet against the box.

"Why are you doing this to me?"

"Amykah, I am not doing anything to you. I'm here to help you," the voice responded cooly.

"Well, if you're really here to help me, then get me the hell out of here!"

"That's what I am trying to do if you would just listen. Look at the cuffs, Amykah, they aren't locked."

"What are you talking about? Of course, they are locked. Don't you think I would have taken them off by now if they weren't locked?" I said to the mysterious voice, rolling my eyes even though I knew he couldn't see me.

"Humor, me," the voice replied.

I brought the cuff close to my face and slowly turned my wrist over, thoroughly examining its surface. How did I not see it before? There was a nearly invisible hinge with a tiny clasp. I pushed the clasp with my fingers, and the cuff popped open. My mouth fell as I stared at my now free wrist. I repeated this process with the cuffs on my opposite wrist and both ankles. Well, at least I was no longer chained, but I was still stuck in this wooden box.

"Okay, now what? Can't you just let me out of the box?" I asked, rubbing my wrists.

"No, it doesn't work that way, Amykah."

"What do you mean it doesn't work that way?" I said slowly through gritted teeth. "You are out there. I am in here. It would seem you could easily open the top up and let me out. Simple."

There was a long pause followed by a sigh.

"You will find a latch behind your head."

"You have got to be kidding me," I muttered under my breath.

I reached my hand above me. As I traced my finger along the joint where the lid met the wall, I ran into something. There is no chance there was a latch there before. It's like the voice talks, and then, as if by magic, things suddenly appear. If I'm going to unlatch this door, I better be ready with something to defend myself just in case whoever was helping wasn't so friendly after all. I grabbed a cuff in one hand, reached for the latch, and pushed. Instantly, I was on my back with a crash. Stunned and a little dizzy from hitting my head, I found myself staring up at a dingy metal ceiling.

Remembering my situation, I scrambled the rest of the way out of the crate, pushing my back up against the wall of the box car, cuff in one hand at the ready. My jaw dropped as the cuff fell to the floor.

"What are *you* doing here?" I asked.

Standing nearly six feet tall, his beautiful chiseled features and piercing icy grey eyes stared back at me. The edges of his lips curled up.

"Hello, Amykah. Let me properly introduce myself. My name is Chase."

He didn't extend his hand. He just stayed where he was. I stood up and brushed myself off. Then, heat rose to my cheeks as I looked at my leather pants and skin-tight tank top, crossing my arms over my body.

"Chase...wait, are you C? As in the C that left me the cryptic note this morning?" I asked.

"That would be me," he said with a bow and a smile, causing my stomach to flutter.

I scanned the box car, while asking, "Where's Tori?"

"She's not here."

"Then where is she? Why are you here? Wait, no, why am *I* here? What the hell is going on?" I asked, pacing every inch of the fifty-foot box car.

"You wouldn't believe me if I told you," he said.

I stopped and squared myself to face him.

"Try me."

He raised his eyebrow and then shook his head with a snicker.

"Ok, you asked for it. You were captured by The Dark Army and are being held in a room strapped to a chair inside the Kesganbern, one of the Dark Institutes. Your mind is currently being controlled by a creature known as a Karekidin, a half-human, half-fallen hybrid manufactured by the Dark. All of this," he said, motioning to the box car and its contents, "is just a projection in your mind carefully crafted by the Karekidin. None of it is real."

I just stared at him blankly, completely speechless.

"I told you you wouldn't believe me," he said matter-of-factly.

"A Karekidin? Why would it be bothering with me? I'm a nobody."

Chase shook his head.

"You are *not* a nobody, Amykah. Karekidins are created for only one purpose: to permanently trap those who would go against the Dark in their own mind. You are a threat to the Dark's very existence. They saw an opportunity to take you out, and they did."

My head hurt trying to piece together everything Chase had told me up to this point.

"So, let me get this straight. I'm not really here. My body is strapped somewhere to a chair with a creature scrambling my brain because I am some kind of threat to the Dark."

"Exactly," Chase said. "Do you remember what the letter from your father said?"

"How do you know about the letter from my father?" I asked, taking a few steps back. "I couldn't find *it* or the book in my apartment. I assumed they weren't real, just another hallucination."

"They are very real and in a safe place," he said with a grin.

"What do you mean they are in a safe place...did you break into my apartment and steal them?" I said, demanding an answer.

He chuckled.

"In a manner of speaking."

This time, I didn't take comfort in his smile because behind it hid something unsettling.

He waved his hand dismissively.

"Never mind, we can talk about it later. Are you ready to get out of here?" he asked.

I crossed my arms and cocked my head to the side.

"And how do you propose we do that?"

"Well, first of all, there is no 'we'. I'm not really here with you. I'm projecting myself into your mind."

It was all too much for me to take and I snapped.

"Why should I believe you, let alone trust you?"

"Excuse me?" he asked, seemingly offended someone would question his intentions.

"You just told me you broke into my apartment and stole from me. How do I know you're even here to help me? Maybe you're the one who put me here in the first place."

He shrugged.

"It seems you have two options. Either you can stay here and let the Karekidin have its way with your mind or you can trust me and get the hell out of this place."

My eyes locked onto his now cold, grey gaze as I crossed my arms. The moment I blinked, Chase vanished, and I was alone. My heart pounded in my chest. I searched the entire box car to see if he had somehow hidden himself from my view, which he clearly had not. I was alone.

"Do you believe me now?" a disembodied voice asked.

"I don't know, maybe you know how to do magic tricks? It doesn't prove I should trust you," I said kicking my boot against the wooden crate. "Alright, then, try and touch me," he dared.

He appeared out of thin air. I stumbled backward, steadying myself on the wall. My heart skipped a beat as I stepped toward him and slowly reached my hand out. It went right through him. I jumped back, pressing myself against the metal wall.

"Proof enough?" Chase asked.

I looked at my trembling hands and then back at him.

"If you still doubt me, open the door and look outside."

Still stunned by the turn of events, I gingerly walked over to the sliding door and wedged myself between it and the door frame. The door's weight proved challenging, but I had enough leverage from my current position. As it opened, the suctioning force nearly yanked me from the boxcar into the rushing scenery.

"How is this not real?" I yelled over the wind as it whipped in my face while keeping a firm grip on the wall.

"Because it's not," he said.

It's as if he whispered it right into my ear. I quickly turned and was face to face with Chase. The sheer closeness of him sent me reeling backward, landing square on my ass.

"I would help you up if I could," he said with a laugh.

I rolled my eyes, made my way off the ground, and stood beside him.

"What do you see, Amykah?"

"Well, um, it's going by pretty fast, but trees, grass, rocks, flowers, a mountain," I paused and looked at him, "I'm not sure how any of this is helping."

He sighed and pointed to the scenery.

"Look closer. What do you notice about those things?"

When I looked again, time slowed. I looked at Chase, then back outside.

"There's a pattern. It's like the scenery keeps repeating itself."

"Now, would that happen in reality?"

"Of course not," I said, staring in disbelief.

"Are you *finally* ready to get out of here?" Chase asked.

I sighed, "Yes, but what do I have to do?"

He gave me a little wink and a smile.

"Jump."

"Are you out of your mind?" I said, ready to send him my most vicious glare, but he had disappeared again.

His voice echoed in my head, saying, "Amykah, I can't do it for you. You have to believe none of this is real and jump. That is your only way out."

This felt like where Neo had to jump in order to discover *The Matrix* wasn't real. But I'm not Neo, and this is definitely *not* a movie. Breathing rapidly, everything in my body screamed no as it shook violently in protest, but then this small, soft voice in the background whispered jump. I walked to the opposite side of the door and pressed my body against the wall with my foot propped up against it to give me a boost. I sprinted toward the door, closed my eyes at the last minute, and jumped.

# CHAPTER 11

A SEARING PAIN PIERCED my head. I tried to open my eyes, but my body wouldn't respond. Maybe I *had* just jumped off a moving train and was now lying in a field broken into pieces. Somewhere no one would find me, where I would just waste away until the vultures and other scavengers came to pick my bones clean.

Just then, a bright light flooded through my closed eyelids. I told my eyes to open, and they slowly lifted in response. As I blinked, the world around me came into focus. I realized I wasn't broken in a field somewhere, but instead, in a room where fluorescent lights reflected white everywhere I looked. Still unable to move anything but my eyes, I saw shiny black leather stretched out in front of me with black boots and brown leather straps around the ankles. I recognized they were my legs, but they felt detached and foreign. My eyes traced their way up my thighs, then shifted to where another brown leather strap secured my wrist to the chair I was sitting in. Was I in the mental hospital again?

I heard a shuffling noise, then a high-pitched whistle followed by something heavy hitting the floor. Intense pain gripped my head. My body seized momentarily. Something wet and thick ran down my cheek while blobs of black viscous matter were splattered on my arms.

Words wouldn't come. All I could do was move my eyes and blink. Then I saw him. He was wiping the same black matter from his machete before carefully returning it to its resting place on his back under his jacket.

I locked eyes with him, wordlessly pleading for him to help me somehow.

"Don't worry, the paralytic agent will wear off quickly," he said, as though reading my mind.

His grey eyes looked me over while quickly unstrapping me from the chair. The pain in my head was subsiding, and my skin started to prickle. I wiggled my fingers and toes as I slowly regained control of my body. I had so many questions, but my mouth was dry, making it difficult to formulate words.

Chase slid one arm behind my back and the other under my legs. Instantly, I was sitting on the edge of the chair with my feet on the floor. The warmth of his arm on my back as he held me upright felt solid and real. But how could I really trust my senses at this point? This could just be another projection. The world started spinning around me. I rested my head on his shoulder and closed my eyes.

"How are you feeling? Do you think you can move yet?" he asked, softly tucking a wayward hair behind my ear then trailing his fingers along my jawline.

I shivered, despite the heat I felt rising inside of me from his touch.

"Are you cold?" he asked, whipping off his jacket to reveal a tight-fitting grey t-shirt clinging to every muscle on his body and placed it around my shoulders.

I avoided eye contact with him, fearing he would read my thoughts.

"I feel like I've been run over by a truck," I finally said, rubbing my head.

While looking down, I noticed Chase's brown boots splattered with some kind of black goo, roughly the same size as the footprints made from the congealed black matter on the floor next to us. My eyes retraced the steps back to the source, where I saw a smooth, pale, disembodied head. Its eyes and mouth had been systematically sewn shut with thick, ragged black threading. Without warning, I leaned over the edge of the chair, where my stomach contents promptly emptied themselves onto the floor. That's when I spied what the head was supposed to be attached to, the now crumpled body on the floor behind the chair. Its black cloak contrasted with the silvery foot-long spikes extending from its wrists while simultaneously camouflaging the blood spatter.

I looked at my arms, swallowing back the bile as my body trembled.

"Is this its blood?"

Chase nodded. He stood up, walked over to the creature's lifeless body, and, with his bare hands, tore off a piece of its cloak and handed it to me. I wiped my mouth and then cleaned off the rest of its blood from my body.

"How can you be so calm?" I said, fighting off waves of nausea.

He looked down at the pile of flesh next to his feet and then at me.

"Amykah, I know this is a lot for you to take in right now, but this is the world as it *actually* is. An unseen world within a world. One most humans can't or don't want to believe exists. That thing was a Karekidin. But, don't worry, it is *very* dead," Chase said, wiping a gloop of black matter I'd missed from my face, seemingly unphased by it all.

Trying to regain my composure, I asked, "What do you mean this is the world as it actually is?".

"There is a plane that coexists within your world, where dark forces are trying to take control of humanity for their own purposes."

I blinked rapidly, trying to process the words he spoke. It sounded very similar to what was in my father's letter.

"Is there anyone trying to stop these dark forces?" I asked.

"Yes, there is an equal opposing force of Light as well as another force that comes directly from humanity itself. A lineage of heroes and heroines who have awakened to their abilities and their role in fighting for humanity. Amykah, you are one of them. That is why you can see the things you see."

"Are you telling me that everything I have seen and heard that I thought were hallucinations, were actually real?"

Chase nodded.

I paused, allowing my mind to absorb and process the information.

"So, you're saying there are forces of Light and Dark battling each other for humanity, and only the awakened ones are fighting back while the rest of the world has no idea it is going on?"

"Basically."

"But how was I awakened?"

"The process was initiated when your father died."

I shook my head with a laugh that ended in a small snort.

"You must really think I'm stupid or something because all of this sounds absolutely insane."

Chase started pacing, obviously bothered by my comment.

"Really? Waking up to discover a Kuza watching you. The messages you've seen everywhere that weren't really there. The demon possession on your bus ride and at the elevator. The Cogere that almost sliced your friend's throat. Being here with me surrounded by the blood of a dead Karekidin. How else would you explain it?"

"I had a psychotic break, and I'm currently in a medically induced coma at the mental institution and... Wait a minute, how could you possibly know all of that happened? You weren't even there...were you?" I said, staring at him in disbelief.

"It doesn't really matter how I know," he started.

I cut him off mid-sentence.

"It matters to me. How do you expect me to trust you?"

"I thought rescuing you from the Karekidin would have earned me some trust, but apparently, I am mistaken." Chase threw his hands in the air with a grunt. "I was at your doctor's office building, the club, and now here. That is how I know about those instances. We have people everywhere, tracking what happens to the Awakened. That's how I got the rest of the information."

"But it still doesn't answer—" I said, but this time Chase quickly cut me off.

"Since you are now an Awakened, the veil has been lifted, and you see everything on our plane and yours."

"Hold on...you just said *our* plane and *yours*. Does that mean you're not from my plane?" I said, judging the distance between me and the door.

He saw my eyes and instantly knew what I was thinking.

"Look, Amykah, I'm here to help you. Why else would I be here? Think about it for a minute. If I wasn't here to protect you, wouldn't I have just left you to the Karekidin?"

He had a point, although a small part of me doubted his intentions.

"You still haven't told me *what* you are," I said, staying firmly planted in the chair, my eyes following him as he moved.

"They didn't tell me you would be this difficult," he mumbled to himself, thinking I couldn't hear him, then continued speaking in his usual tone. "I can see we are not going anywhere until you get some answers," he sighed. He paced the room as he continued, "I'm what you call an In-Between or a Grey One. Since we don't have much time, here's the short version. As I said before, there is the Light One and the Dark One, and each has an army fighting for the rights to humanity. We, the In-Between, have no allegiance to either side and are fighting on behalf of humanity for its freedom. A few years ago, I was assigned to watch you since your father was one of the higher orders. We discovered The Dark had been hunting him, trying to take him out. That's when we realized we needed to keep an eye on you too." Chase paused, choosing his next words carefully, "After he died, the lineage was activated and you were awakened. But you had no training and no clue what was happening to you. So, your mom, based on what she saw with her unawakened eyes, did the only thing she knew to do and took you to Harbor View."

"Ok, so let's say I believe everything you just said. It's been a year since my father died. Why is all this happening now?" I had to admit I was curious about the answer. So were the two warring minds inside of me. One was certain I had completely lost touch with reality and was resting peacefully strapped to a bed in Harbor View. The other wanted to believe what Chase was saying because if it were true, it meant I was never broken in the first place, which would change the entire context of my life.

Chase sat down next to me.

"They pumped you full of meds for six months in that hospital and convinced you everything you were experiencing could be chalked up to a break from reality in your psyche. Once you were out, you continued to numb your abilities with medication and alcohol. I had to do something. We couldn't have you like that any longer. We needed you to wake up."

"What do you mean 'we' needed you to wake up? What did you do?" I questioned as my spine straightened and muscles tensed.

Chase raised his eyebrows. His lips curled up into a little smirk, seemingly proud of what he was about to reveal.

"I switched out your medication both at home and at the pharmacy. The pills you've been taking are placebos."

"You did what?" I said, digging my nails into the edge of the chair infuriated once again by his apparent violation of my life.

He glanced at the door and then back at me, saying, "Can you please keep your voice down? We really don't want to let them know we are here. Not yet, anyway."

"When did you change out the pills at my apartment?" I asked through gritted teeth.

"A few weeks ago," he said with a hint of remorse.

"So, this whole time I thought I was losing my mind, it was because of you? Did you ever think maybe I don't *want* to be awakened? That I just want to have a normal life?" I said, my throat tightening with each word.

"Amykah, it wasn't my choice. It was time for you to pick up where your dad left off," he said, reaching his finger behind his ear. His body suddenly went rigid as an iridescent film appeared over his eyes, reflecting reds, greens, and blues in the light.

I waved my hand in front of his zombie-like face.

"Chase, what is going on? Chase...Chase..."

He held up one finger to his lips. That's when I saw a small, ridged metal plate attached behind his ear with hair-like wires extending into his skull. He pressed a button, and the iridescent film disappeared from his eyes while his body relaxed.

"What the hell just happened?" I asked.

Chase frowned, shifting his gaze toward the door.

"Amykah, we don't have time for any more questions. I will explain everything later, but we have to go now. It's not safe for us to stay here," he said, holding out his hand as his grey eyes stormed.

I surveyed the room with congealed black matter sprayed all over the white walls, chair, and floor from the motionless, beheaded creature. I took Chase's hand, and he pulled me up to him. My breath caught.

"Where are we, and what exactly are we going to do?" I asked, looking up at him through my lashes, my heart pounding.

"Remember, I said no more questions," he said softly, placing his hands on my shoulders.

"That's the last one. I promise," I said, hopeful he would give in.

He sighed as a slight grin crossed his lips.

"Okay, last one. We are technically still in the warehouse, but we are really in a pocket of space-time existing outside of your world in one of the Dark Institutes. The Dark has Institutes like this all over the World," he paused, fixing his gaze on me while still holding my shoulders.

Despite all the questions bubbling up in my head, I was unable to speak. I couldn't take my eyes off of him.

"We are going to be alright, Amykah. You can trust me. You need to see for yourself who you really are. That's where I'm taking you."

A wave of calm washed over me as all my questions and fears floated away. He grabbed his jacket that had fallen off my shoulders from the chair, and in one seamless motion, Chase had it back on, never breaking eye contact with me. He took my hand and led me to the door. I followed, mesmerized, as if I weren't in control of my own actions.

"You ready?"

I nodded, still spellbound by him. Chase silently opened the door and slid through, pulling me with him.

# CHAPTER 12

MY EYES ADJUSTED TO the dimly lit hallway. The outline of light grey doors spaced evenly against the dark grey walls, stretched as far as my eyes could see. In one direction, soft light projected patches on the floor at random intervals creating a pathway that led to a promising yet barely visible glow at the end of the hallway. In the other direction, nothing but darkness.

Chase's arm grazed my side when he reached behind me to close the door. My breath caught again from his touch. Heat radiated from his body, causing my skin to tingle. His hand reached around to the small of my back, pulling me closer. The pounding of my heart was so loud I thought for sure he would hear it. I opened my mouth to speak. He pressed his finger lightly against my lips.In any other situation, it would be obvious the guy was hitting on me, but with Chase, nothing was ever obvious. He leaned in, and as his cheek brushed mine, my body quaked in response.

"Don't move. The lights are motion-activated," he said, his breath tickling my ear.

He leaned back slightly, leaving only inches between us.

"We have to move quickly through this hall if we don't want to get caught," he whispered.

The sweet smell of his breath was intoxicating. I couldn't think straight, let alone speak. Sure, he was handsome in that movie star leading man sort of way, but there was something else. Something I couldn't quite put my finger on. I closed my eyes and held my breath, shutting him out momentarily. Just like that, the fog obscuring my mind lifted, allowing my thoughts to come rushing back in. My free will was no longer subverted. Tension seized my body. My eyes flew open.

"Wait," I whispered. "No, I'm not ready. I still have so many questions."

The heat of his hand pulsated on my arm as his gaze intensified.

"Amykah, I want to answer all of your questions," he spoke slowly, "and I will, just not right now. We have to go."

Once again, his words made my questions disappear like a puff of smoke. My body relaxed and all I could muster was a, "Mmmm hmmm."

He grabbed my hand, and we took off at a sprint before I could protest. I was doing my best to keep up as the lights sprang to life one by one, spotlighting us when we ran under them. Door after door went by in a blur. A small light cast shadows on the floor in front of us. I made the mistake of following the light to its origination. I stopped. Through the glass, I saw a man who looked vaguely familiar strapped to a chair just like the one I had left. The creature had its icepick-like extensions buried into his skull. I knew him from somewhere. Searching my memories, I found the answer. On the nightly news a few days ago, they reported a Congressman taking a sudden leave of absence due to a family emergency.

"Oh my God, that's the Congressman. You have to save him," I said, opening the door to the small room, dragging Chase with me.

Chase's eyes went wide. In an instant, I was pushed up against the wall. The cold concrete on my back and the pressure of his arm across my chest made it hard to breathe. His eyes were dark.

"What are you doing, trying to get us killed?"

I could never have imagined a whisper could be so loud.

"But...it was the Congressman. He has a family—we have to save him."

Chase positioned himself directly in front of me.

"I don't care if it was your mother in there. My job is to keep *you* safe, which you are making very difficult right now."

A cold spread through me as my hands started to shake.

"Well, we can't just leave him there," I pleaded.

"That is precisely what we are going to do."

Who was *this* Chase standing before me, because I didn't like him very much. All I saw was hardness and sharp angles in his face.

Somewhere behind us, we heard the distinct sound of a light flickering on. Chase looked back at the darkened hallway behind us, and every muscle in his body tensed.

"We need to go right now," he ground out, grabbing my hand and pulling me down the hallway.

Not knowing who or what was after us, we ran, trying every door in hopes of finding one unlocked. Chase looked over his shoulder into the darkness as the buzz of lights flickering to life edged closer.

Finally, one gave way. I rushed into the room with Chase on my heels. He quickly pulled me to the floor and we pressed our backs against the door. I held my breath. We waited as the light outside flickered to life.

There was a slow, steady click, click, click against the ground. A large shadowy figure crossed on the floor before us then disappeared. Suddenly, a heavy weight slammed against the door, shaking our bodies. A gasp escaped my lips, immediately followed by a soft, firm hand on my mouth. I looked at Chase while the creature threw itself against the door for a second time. Then silence.

A shadow rose once again, and this time, I could clearly see the outline of horns before it completely obscured the light with its massive body. Clicking its talons on the window one by one, it snorted, and a bone-chilling, high-pitched screech filled the air as it slowly dragged its hooked claws down the glass. The shadow disappeared with a thud and then silence. I looked at Chase, my eyes wide. We waited for the hum of the next light to come to life as the one outside our door went dark. Chase released my mouth, and I exhaled.

"Are you okay?" he whispered.

"I am most certainly *not* okay. I just found out a whole other world exists within ours. Light and Dark are vying for humanity, and I somehow play a role in all of it. Humans are being captured and held captive. And we were just chased by whatever that thing was..."

He pressed himself against the door, sliding up enough to peer out the window.

"I'm pretty sure that was a Cogere," he said, sinking back down beside me.

I shook my head.

"How can any of this be real?" I paused, waiting for his response, and when nothing came, I asked, "Isn't this the part where you are supposed to offer me a choice? Take the blue pill, and the story ends. I wake up in my bed and believe whatever I want to believe. Take the red pill, and I stay in Wonderland to see how deep the rabbit hole goes. Well, I choose the blue pill. I want to go back to sleep," I said, holding my hand out.

Chase's eyes were blank as he shrugged.

"I have no idea what you are talking about, Amykah. I don't have any pills, red or blue. But whether you want this or not, the choice has already been made for you. It's up to you to decide what you are going to do with it. If you do nothing, you will most certainly end up back with the Karekidin scrambling your brain, as you so eloquently put it earlier, or worse, dead. If you choose to embrace who you are, you help save humanity and become the heroine of your story. Which path do you want to take?"

"Is that really even a choice?" I asked with a huff.

Chase stood up, offering me his hand. "There is always a choice, even when one is not evident. You have to choose the path with the consequences you can live with."

I took his hand and let him pull me to my feet.

"I still don't think that's much of a choice."

Chase's face became solemn.

"Amykah, I need to prepare you for what's coming next."

I chuckled. "It can't be worse than what we've already been through."

Pursing his lips together as though trying to find the right words, he finally spoke.

"What you are about to see is much worse. They have your friends, Tori and Lexi. I am not sure what state they will be in when we see them, but I promise we will save them *after* I show you the Book."

I was barely listening to him while my mind wandered to the possible scenarios that could be worse than what we'd already been through.

"Well, I wouldn't really call Tori a friend. Wait, what? What do you mean they have my friends and you're not sure what state they will be in?"

"They kidnapped Lexi from the club to set a trap for you and Tori. Both of them have been captured. I've been busy rescuing you, so, I don't..."

I cut him off.

"Then *why* would we have to see a stupid Book before saving them?"

"Because that stupid Book is the key that will prove to you who you truly are. If we rescue your friends first, it will be a blood bath. The Dark will know we are here, and we'll have zero shot at the Book." He got quiet and looked at the floor, which was unlike Chase, as he continued. "But, and this is a big but, to get to the Book, we first have to go through the Lab."

"The Lab?" I asked.

"Every Dark Institute has a Lab. It's where they perform their experiments on humans. No one should ever have to go through these experiments, let alone witness them. The Lab is where your friends are being held." He looked up, his eyes meeting mine. "Amykah, we have to go through the Lab to get to the hallway that will lead us to the Book, which means we will have to leave your friends behind. But I promise you, we will come back and save them."

"I don't think I can do that," I said, my breath quickening.

Chase stepped toward me and lifted my hand in his. His grey eyes shone as he looked into mine, and his voice was soothing and calm.

"Amykah, you have more strength and courage than you know," he paused, looking down at his hand still holding mine, then back into my eyes. "There are two things I need you to do for me. First, you have to keep a hold of my hand at all times while we are in the Lab, and second, no matter what you see, you *must* keep moving."

"If you wanted to hold my hand so badly, you should take me out on a proper date without all the monsters, death, and gore," I said with a sly grin, unsure of where this newfound boldness came from.

"Maybe another time," he said, flashing me a smile in return. "Holding my hand will shield you from their vision."

I couldn't keep a straight face as I spoke. "How can holding your hand keep them from seeing me? It's not like you have some magical powers." I waited for his response. When it became clear he wasn't refuting my statement, I dropped his hand and took a step back. "Do you have magical powers?"

"Look, as Greys," he hesitated, "we have some unique abilities, and one of them happens to be the ability to shield. By holding my hand, the ability extends to you. You have abilities, too, you know. You just haven't developed them yet."

I crossed my arms and narrowed my eyes. "You like to use the word shield, but that's just a fancy way to say you basically can make yourself invisible. Is there anything else you want to tell me about your abilities?" I said, gritting my teeth.

He stepped closer to me, and this time, I didn't back away.

"No, that's about the extent of them," he said.

It's interesting how he used the word about, but I didn't press the issue. It was clear Chase wasn't going to tell me anything more than he thought was necessary. I was on a need-to-know basis, which didn't sit well with me.

He held his hand out to me, asking, "So what are you choosing, Amykah?"

"I guess I'll take the red pill and see how deep this rabbit hole goes," I said, reaching for his outstretched hand.

Chase shook his head.

"I still don't understand what taking a blue or red pill has to do with any of this. All I need to know is if you're ready to step into your birthright and see reality for what it is?"

Taking a step closer to him, I sighed, resigned to my fate. "Yes."

A smile spread across his lips. He opened the door and poked his head out, checking to make sure it was clear. He pulled me into the hallway next to him. Ahead, a bright light poured through a doorway, which I could only assume was the entrance to the Lab. We ran toward the light, and when we neared the threshold, Chase looked over his shoulder at me.

"Remember, whatever you do, don't let go of my hand."

# CHAPTER 13

A S WE ENTERED THE light, I froze. The walls were floor-to-ceiling glass stretching at least twenty feet high. Lining the lower floor were glass cages filled with humans and other human-like creatures. One was lying on the floor of his cage, picking at his skin as black pus oozed from it. Another bared its teeth and pounded its claws on the glass. Still, another was scratching her eyes until her fingers were covered in blood.

Above the cages, more glass revealed a training room where what looked like people in all-black uniforms were sparring with one another. Some had weapons, while others were the weapons themselves. The glass opposite the training room held desks where human and not-so-human things were diligently studying.

I directed my gaze toward the smell of burnt flesh in the center of the room. There were five white elevated tables, which made the contrasting crimson blood dripping from one of them even more horrifying. Each operating table held a tray of tools. I recognized some of them. Scalpel, forceps, clamps, and other instruments I had never seen before. There was one object that looked like it could be used for spreading something large apart, and next to it was a giant peeler. I shuddered when I couldn't stop my mind from thinking of what they might be used for.

Bags full of various colored liquids were mounted about five feet above the table on a rectangular metal frame secured by posts welded at each corner. One was full of black liquid, which looked similar to the blood of the Karkedin Chase had killed, while the others held clear, yellow, and a fizzing green liquid. From each bag hung a pencil-sized needle attached to a tube.

At either end of the table, chains dangled down with different implements attached to them, one of them being cuffs. White lab coats surrounded a few of the tables. I couldn't tell if they were human or something else. I assumed if they were surrounding a table, someone or something must be lying on it.

Chase squeezed my hand and pointed to the doorway at the far right end of the Lab. Just above it was a wall of mirrored glass extending the entire length of the room. It seemed like the kind of place where higher-ups would be to ensure they could see everything went according to plan while avoiding getting their hands dirty.

My legs were unwilling to move as I stared at the gauntlet we had to navigate. I felt a tightening on my hand. I lowered my eyes to find Chase staring at me. He flipped his hand over and began moving his index and pointer fingers like they were walking. I nodded and held his hand tightly, remembering as long as I did, nothing could see us.

We walked past some of the glass cages, and I couldn't help but stare. These were humans. A homeless man sat in the corner of his prison, rocking. In the next one, a young girl, no more than fifteen, banged her head against the glass with blood smearing at her every touch. Then, my heart stopped. It was Tori, sitting on the floor, still wearing her green cut-off tank with her back against the wall, eyes unblinking. One of her eyes was black and swollen. I also noticed several cuts with dried blood all over her face and body. Her camo pants were torn as well. Even though I didn't really know or like Tori all that much, I couldn't stand to see her hurt and looking so broken.

I pulled Chase toward the cage holding Tori captive, pleading to him with my eyes. He shook his head no, trying to pull me away. I pulled back, my eyes stern and my body unmoving.

"Remember, Amykah, we need to keep moving. We'll help her later," his voice echoed in my head while his lips remained motionless.

I stepped back, releasing his hand, which he quickly grabbed and held tight.

"Amykah, I told you not to let go," his voice reverberating in my head.

Heat flooded my face. My eyes sharpened as I stared him down.

"Look, I didn't tell you I could project my thoughts into another person's mind because you were already dealing with so much. I really didn't think it was important at the time, but clearly, I was wrong," he said inside my head.

I remained unmoved.

"I'm sorry. I'm sure there are a lot more things I haven't told you that I will get in trouble for, but we are pressed for time right now. Can we go?"

With teeth clenched and fire still in my eyes, I nodded.

We edged our way toward the door, skirting the center of the room. That's when I saw her. Her red hair cascading off the end of the table while her pale body dressed in grey scrubs, lay motionless. One of the white coats reached for a tube extending from a bag of white liquid and jabbed the needle into Lexi's lifeless arm. I glimpsed its face. My mouth fell open upon discovering it was a human. He pushed his grey hair away from his face and then raised Lexi's shirt, exposing her abdomen. Opposite the human was another white coat with its back to me. A tentacle snaked from under the sleeve, wrapping around a scalpel. As it raised the scalpel, ready to make a cut, I couldn't stop myself from screaming.

Instantly, my mouth was covered. Chase pulled me tight against his chest. The creature set down the scalpel and made a chiding sound toward another white coat. A chill ran up my spine as the one it communicated with turned around.

"Don't move, don't even breathe," Chase's voice filled my head.

My body tensed as I held my breath.

It definitely was not human. It fell to the floor, slithering towards us when it suddenly stopped and rose on its tail, towering over me but coming eye to eye with Chase's six-foot frame. Its human-shaped head, eyes like a snake, and two slits where a nose would be, sniffed at the air. Without warning, it unhinged its jaw like a Russian doll projecting layer after layer of razor-sharp teeth. The scent of rotting flesh infiltrated my nose while green drops oozed from its fangs. It flicked its tongue in the air inches away from Chase's face. Then, sniffed at the air once again, satisfied there was nothing, retracted its teeth into its mouth. It fell to the floor and slinked back to where Lexi lay.

My body shook uncontrollably as Chase lifted me off the floor, carrying me with his hand firmly over my mouth toward the doorway that had been our destination. Wet, hot tears streamed down my face, blurring the tables and glass cages we passed.

I heard the click of a door, and Chase finally let me go. My knees gave way when my feet touched the ground. I collapsed to the floor.

"We must go back. We have to save them," I said, looking up at him through my tear-soaked lashes.

Chase blocked the door with his body. "We can't, Amykah. At least not yet. I need you to pull yourself together before we can continue."

I slowly got to my feet, wiping away the tears while surveying the room. We were in a supply closet, amidst soiled linens, barrels filled with the same colored liquids hanging in the bags in the Lab, bandages and gauze of all shapes and sizes, and used surgical tools. My stomach lurched at the sight of it. I swallowed hard, keeping the sick from rising any further.

Diverting my attention from the sights and smells surrounding me, I focused on Chase.

"Can't you just use some of your abilities to sneak them out of here undetected?"

He walked over to me and gently wiped the remaining tears from my face.

"I would have to kill everyone and everything at the table to free Lexi. I'm pretty sure *that* would be detected," he said.

"So, we are just going to leave them there, having God knows what being done to them?" My shoulders slumped. The knowing I had felt earlier began to slip away, and the fear crept back in. "Chase, what if I'm not who you think I am? What if I can't do what you think I can?"

"Well, then, I guess humanity will fall to the Dark and be damned for all eternity."

I stepped back, my eyes wide.

"Too soon for jokes?" he said with a laugh. "What I think doesn't matter. It is in your blood, in your bones, and just plainly who you are. Amykah, you are a force to be reckoned with...well, maybe not right this minute," he said, pausing as he smiled, "but it is within you. It is your birthright. Once you see who you *really* are and what you can do," he shook his head, "all I can say is I hope I am still on your good side."

Leaning into him, he wrapped his arms around me. I felt safe for the first time in a long time. I closed my eyes, wishing this was all just a bad dream and I'd wake up in my bed. When I opened them, those piercing grey eyes looked back at me.

I stepped away from his embrace, flushed and shaky.

"Tell me more about this Book," I said, changing the subject.

He grinned, making me question if he knew what I was thinking.

"It's called the Book of the Dark. All the lineages of humans that are in some way meant to take down the Dark are detailed in the book. There is one list of Potentials whose abilities are dormant and another list of Awakened whose abilities have been activated."

"And my name is in there? Why do we need to see the book if we already know I am Awakened?" I asked, avoiding eye contact and fidgeting with my hands.

"The Book not only shows if the person is Awakened, but also details their abilities. That's one of the reasons we need to get to the Book, for you to discover what your abilities are. Which by the way, the clock is ticking, and we need to get going. The sooner you see the book, the sooner we can save your friends."

He put one hand on the door and the other stretched out toward me. I grasped it as we left the supply room's relative safety and entered the darkness once again.

# CHAPTER 14

T HERE WAS A STARK difference between this hallway and the last. Concrete surrounded us on all sides and there were no doors lining the walls in case we needed to make a quick escape. The only perceptible light came from the Lab where I had reluctantly left Lexi and Tori. Facing the darkness, a chill penetrated my bones. Something didn't feel quite right. A thought tugged at the corner of my mind, refusing to let go until it had a satisfactory response.

"Why didn't you use your shielding ability before? In the other hallway?" I asked pointedly.

"What do you mean?" he said, looking into the darkness.

"Well, in the other hallway, why didn't you use your shielding ability when the creature was after us? Why make all the fuss of running and hiding in a room?"

He tilted his head and floated his gaze toward the ceiling, seemingly concentrating on something important. After what felt like five minutes of silence, more like thirty seconds, he looked me square in the eye and finally spoke.

"It wouldn't have made a difference. We still would have triggered the lights, indicating someone or something was there. It doesn't shield us from human sensors."

He turned away from me, flicked on a small flashlight he had pulled from one of his many pockets and began walking. It irritated me how he always seemed to have an explanation that made logical sense at the ready. I felt he was giving me half-truths, just enough information to appease my curiosity, while at the same time artfully leaving out anything he didn't want me to know.

"What about this hallway?" I asked, following him.

"What about it?" he countered.

"Aren't you worried they might find us here?"

"Not particularly," he said without a glance in my direction.

"And why is that?"

He stopped suddenly. I ran straight into the back of him, almost knocking us both over. He slowly turned around to face me.

"Because there is only one person who would have reason to come down this hallway, and *he* is not here. And by the way, the more questions you ask, the longer it will take to get to the Book and the longer it will take to save your friends."

He spun on his heels and strode into the darkness. I jogged to catch up to him.

"And how do you know *he* is not here?"

He turned his head and pointed to the small, ridged metal plate attached behind his ear I had seen earlier. He pressed a button on the device. The wires embedded in his skull retracted as the device sprouted tiny centipede legs and scurried down his arm into his waiting palm, where it promptly turned back into an inanimate object he slid into his pocket.

"What the hell was that thing?" I asked, my stomach seizing at the thought of a little creature inserting wires into his brain.

"It's a simple communication device. It's how I knew the layout of this place, about your friends, and that the General wouldn't be here."

I raised my eyebrow.

"The General? Does this General have a name, or is he just called The General?"

He let out another heavy sigh.

"You know, the more answers I give you, the more questions you seem to have."

"Well, wouldn't you? Have questions, I mean. You don't seem like the kind of guy who would tolerate not having all the answers. Why should *I* be any different?"

He paused, looking at me with hypnotic grey eyes, quickening my pulse.

"Fair enough," he said with a shrug and continued walking. "The Dark has a hierarchy. At the top is the Dark One. No one has ever seen his face except his Generals. The Generals are the right hand of the Dark One. They're in charge of carrying out his orders, and no, they do not have names. They are typically Pure Bloods from our plane, but sometimes a human can rise to that level if they are particularly powerful and loyal to the Dark."

"Pure Bloods, like in *Harry Potter*?" I asked, trying to give context to what he was explaining.

"I don't know who Henry Potter is or if he is a Pure Blood," Chase said.

I laughed.

"It's *Harry Potter*, and it's not a person; it's a book. Don't you read books or watch movies?"

"I don't have time for such nonsense," he said, shaking his head. "May I continue?"

"Please do," I said with a flourish of my hand, giving him my permission even though he wasn't asking for it.

"A Pure Blood is one whose blood has not been contaminated with human blood. And to answer the question I know you will ask, Pure Bloods can become contaminated in two ways. The first is by creating a hybrid, mixing human blood with a being from my plane, whether it be Dark, Light, or Grey. The second is when a child is conceived between our kinds, which goes against our laws. Can I finish this history lesson at a later time?"

"I guess," I said, although I had a zillion questions about the information he just told me.

As we walked, Chase's light illuminated the next few feet in front of us. There were long stretches of concrete, then a corner, followed by yet more long stretches of concrete with more turns. It felt like we slowly descended with each turn, heading deeper into the darkness. When we rounded another corner, an amber hue coated the walls, ceiling, and floor. I stopped for a moment. My body tensed. A shiver raced up my spine, causing the hairs on my neck to stand up.

We rounded the next corner and promptly ran into a dead end.

"What the hell?" I said, shaking off his hand.

I ran to the wall and pushed on it, hoping to find some secret door, but the concrete was cold, hard, and unyielding. Chase's light followed me wherever I went. I checked every wall with the same result. My chest tightened, and my breathing became shallow. I scanned over every inch of concrete and found nothing. I heard a muffled laugh behind me. I slowly turned around to see Chase standing with his hand covering his mouth.

"You think this is funny?" I snapped.

"Well, yeah, a little," he said with a crooked grin.

"Now what?" I said, slumping against the wall.

"Amykah, nothing is ever as it seems. You would do well to remember that."

And with that, he walked over to the wall. He waved his hand in front of it, uttering words under his breath in a different language I couldn't understand. He stood back, and a door appeared where the previously solid concrete wall had been.

"How did you do that? No wait, let me guess, it's just another one of your abilities you've conveniently forgot to tell me about," I said, moving toward the door.

"It's like I told you earlier. I was given all the details of this building, where I would find the Book, how to get us in, et cetera. It's really no big deal. I wasn't hiding it from you."

I looked him up and down, letting his advice, that nothing is ever as it seems, sink in. I wondered if that included him as well. He caught me staring at him.

On the off chance he could read my thoughts, I pointed to the door, asking, "Was that some kind of magical spell you did to make the door appear?"

"I guess you could call it that," he said with a shrug and a smile.

My attention turned toward the enormity of the door. I marveled at its beauty and slid my hand over the wood that seemed to tell a story. At the top was an amorphous cloud, and from it sprang two swirls, one light and one dark. The two swirls blended together, creating the three: light, dark, and grey. From the three came a multitude of carvings in the thousands, including: humans, creatures, the universe, angels, demons, the elements, animals, plants, and images I'd never before seen. Another striking feature I noticed about this particular door, was it didn't have a handle.

"And, how exactly do you propose we get in?" I said pointing to where a door handle should be.

"You wouldn't believe me if I told you. You're just going to have to trust me," he said matter of fact.

He took my hand and started reaching for the door. A thrumming coursed through my veins as my vision blurred. He placed his hand on the image of the three: light, dark, and grey. It dissolved into sand underneath his touch. I pulled my hand out of his and the door became solid once again. Chase looked at his hand, and then at me, quickly dropping his arm to his side.

"What was that?" I said, still reeling from the experience.

"Oh, yeah. I forgot to tell you. We are going to walk through the door, and you may feel a little funny while the atoms are being manipulated, but it can't hurt you unless you let go of my hand," he said, taking my hand again and holding it tightly.

Unsure if I wanted to know the answer, I asked, "What would happen?"

"You'd be stuck inside the door and likely suffocate to death," he said with a smirk.

I glared at him.

"That little piece of information would have been nice to know *before* you tried to take me through the door the first time, don't you think?"

Just to make a point, I latched onto his hand so hard he grimaced.

"You told me what would happen if I let go," I said returning his smirk with one of my own.

Chase put his palm against the door. The thrumming pulsed through my body, blurring my vision once again. His touch changed the molecules into a whirling spiral of sand, transforming the door into a portal.

He looked back, locking eyes with me, "Whatever you do, don't let go of my hand."

I nodded.

Chase moved forward, and his body disappeared into the shifting sands with only his lower arm and hand intact, still holding tightly onto mine. I entered the door, and it was like being in the center of a sandstorm as glistening white particles swirled around my body. I could see nothing else. The next thing I knew, I was on the other side and the door was solid once again. I released Chase's hand and collapsed to the floor in utter exhaustion.

I cautiously propped myself up, my vision returning while the thrumming faded.

"How is that even possible?"

"You can't even imagine half of what is possible in this world," he said, smiling with his hand outstretched.

I swatted his hand away and quickly stood up, dusting myself off.

"I'm still mad at you for conveniently forgetting to mention...well, pretty much everything." I looked Chase up and down. All I really know about him is he is a Grey from another plane with abilities he likes to keep secret. He said he was assigned to me, but by whom? Who is he working for, and to what end? What do they, whoever they are, get by waking me up?

"Why are you looking at me like that?"

"Like what?" I said, avoiding his piercing gaze. Those questions would have to wait for another time. I turned my back to him and looked into the darkness. "What is this place?"

The room suddenly came to life as flames licked the air one by one from torches lining the walls, revealing a floor-to-ceiling library in their fiery glow. A magnificent grand staircase with a deep scarlet pathway beckoned at the far end of the room. Two sets of stairs split in opposite directions off the main landing, each allowing access to either side of the upstairs balcony. A gargoyle stood watch atop each post, poised for action. Its claws tightly clutched the granite, waiting to pounce, while its eyes judged whether or not you were worthy enough to pass.

Corridors extended like spokes in every direction off the main room. Each one was shrouded in darkness and led to more rooms holding who-knows-what kind of dark hidden secrets. Tucked away on the main floor were alcoves, too many to count, concealing mysterious objects in their shadowy depths. A larger-than-life desk sat in the center of the room. The wood was carved as ornately as the door, with similar symbols, designs, and pictures telling the same story. Papers were piled on the desk and floor, but different from the kind of paper I was used to seeing. It was unlined and thicker with ragged edges. I picked up one of the pages inked with symbols in a language I didn't recognize.

"How does a place like this even exist? I would think something of this magnitude would get noticed," I said, taking in the vastness of the space.

Chase ducked from one alcove to another.

"It doesn't really exist in your world. Remember, I told you earlier we are outside the confines of your reality. The door leading back from the lab into the warehouse is the gateway between your world and this plane."

I stroked the leathery textured paper between my fingers.

"So, we are on a different plane of existence right now?" I asked, with the realization I would be committed immediately if anyone outside of this room heard those words come out of my mouth,

"You know you are holding a piece of paper made from flesh, right?" Chase said with a smirk hurrying into another shadowy alcove.

I promptly threw the paper and watched it fall to the floor with a soft plunk.

"Amykah, can you please focus? We need to find the Book."

He dashed over to the desk and began rummaging through the drawers.

"Um, could you narrow it down a bit?" I said, looking around at the thousands of volumes lining the walls.

"It's not just any book. It will be large, bound in..." he paused and looked at me, like he was trying to decide what to say next, "Um, leather, let's just call it leather. It will likely be kept somewhere special, away from other books. There should be an empty ink well with..." another pause, "a writing implement of sorts with it."

It made the most sense for me to go upstairs and check for the Book while Chase was looking downstairs. I headed toward the grand staircase but was stopped in my tracks. I took a few sideways steps to the left, then a few steps to the right. The gargoyle's eyes followed me. To ensure it wasn't a figment of my imagination, I took a few more steps to the right, and that's when I saw it.

A small nook was nestled under the staircase that I would have missed completely had I not been trying to avoid the gargoyle's scrutiny. The Book was bound in black leather; at least, that's what I was telling myself it was. It had a faint glow and a subtle odor of rotting fruit. My body buzzed as I neared the book. An empty ink well with an interesting device, which I could only assume was a pen, sat next to it. The hairs on my arm pricked when I picked up the pen. It was made of silver. One end came to a double-headed point with grooves leading from the hollow shaft where ink could be held. I flipped it over to examine the other end when a tiny hidden razor sliced into my palm. I dropped the pen, but it didn't hit the floor instead, it hovered just above it. The reasonable thing to do would be to turn around and run away. However, today, it seems I must have left my reason on my nightstand next to the empty bottle of vodka.

I watched the pen fly up to meet my palm, attracted to the blood trickling out of my cut. Like a vampire at a blood bank, it drank, sucking the blood up into the shaft. Once it was full, the bleeding stopped, and the edges of the cut drew back together. The pen glided back to the table, settling next to the ink well, a drop of my blood still glistening on the tip of the razor.

Stepping out from under the staircase, I scanned the room for Chase. He wasn't anywhere to be found. Just as I was about to call for him, the Book pulled at me, inviting me to come back. It had begun to glow. I ignored it; however, its advances became more demanding. The book started to pulsate and pain shot up my arm from where the razor had cut me. The surges of pain I felt fell into sync with the pulsing of the Book. The cut opened, and my palm began bleeding.

I screamed as the pain intensified.

Chase raced over to me, then stopped short when he saw the Book. He was entranced. I waved my hands in front of his eyes. He blinked rapidly, shaking his head.

"That's it. The Book of the Dark," he said, his gaze fixed upon the Book.

"Yeah, I kind of figured that out, but we have a bigger problem."

I shoved my blood-covered hand in front of his face.

He ran back to the desk, cursing under his breath along the way until he found what he was looking for. A piece of cloth that could be made into a makeshift tourniquet for my hand. He skillfully wrapped my palm, minimizing the bleeding.

"What the hell happened?"

With the pain still surging in my arm, I told him the sequence of events.

"How do I make it stop?" I asked through clenched teeth.

"I don't know. I've never heard of anything like this happening before. But if the pain and bleeding started when you ignored the Book, maybe you need to go to it."

My muscles tensed as I took a step toward the Book. The pulsing slowed, and the pain lessened. I took another step, now only a few feet away. A steady glow returned to the Book. The pain now a memory; I unwrapped my hand. The edges of the cut had knitted back together. I held it up for Chase to see.

His eyes grew wide.

"I don't know what to tell you, Amykah. I've only ever heard about the Book of the Dark. I've never seen one in person."

"What do you mean you've never seen one? I thought there was only *one* Book of the Dark."

"Technically, there is one original Book of the Dark that is kept by the Dark One himself. All others are basically copies of the original. There is a copy of the Book at every Dark Institute. It is the primary way the Dark One communicates with his Generals. And by the looks of what happened to you, I'd venture a guess they can only communicate with the Dark One in blood."

I swayed as the Book commanded me to come closer. Shuffling my feet on the floor, I complied and inched toward it.

"So if my name *is* in there, then the Dark One and every single General around the world would know about it?"

"Yes," Chase said softly.

I stared at the Book, and the thought of my name actually being in it weighed heavy on me. I swallowed hard against the dryness in my throat.

"How can you be sure my name is in there?"

Chase hesitated before saying, "I know it is. The leader of the Greys is privy to the information found in both the Book of the Dark and the Book of the Light."

My jaw dropped.

"Wait, did you just say there is a Book of the Light?"

"Yes. It's basically the inverse of the Book of the Dark. The Book of the Light has all the names of potentials and awakened who will likely follow the Dark. But that's not important now. What *is* important is you open the Book, find your name, and your destiny," he said, giving me a gentle yet firm nudge toward it.

"Well, there's no pressure there," I said, pushing him back. He lost his balance, and a giant grin spread across my face.

I took a deep breath and put one foot in front of the other. The glow intensified with my approach. I found myself standing in front of the Book once again.

"What if I don't want to know? What if I can't be the Amykah Grayson written in that Book?"

I felt lightheaded. My knees buckled. Chase's hands gripped my shoulders from behind, keeping me upright on my feet. He spun me around to face him. My mouth went dry. I felt a lump growing in my throat and a burning in my eyes.

"You already *are* the Amykah Grayson in that Book, whether you want to believe it or not. It's not a choice you get to make. The question is, are you going to *become* her? Because it's a whole lot better for this World and Humanity if you do."

I reached my hand toward the Book. Blue arcs of light shot from it and connected to my hand. The hairs on my arm stood up. I backed away shaking my head slowly.

"Can't you just do it for me?"

"Stop stalling, Amykah. You need to see it for yourself. Just open the Book and find the letter G for Grayson. "

I cleared my throat while I stretched my trembling hand toward the Book. My fingers burned, touching the cover. I pulled my hand away, inspecting the damage—just a few small blisters.

"Is it normal for it to burn whoever touches it?"

"Well, it is The Book of the Dark, so..." he said with a shrug.

I shook my hands and threw open the Book with a thunk. Thankfully, the internal pages provided only a slight sting compared to the intense burn of the cover. There were hundreds of names. Every name had a number beside it.

"Why are some names glowing and others aren't?"

"If the name is glowing, it means the human has been awakened. They could be at any stage of their awakening. You're an unusual case. Typically, the Awakened know their abilities and have been prepped by the lineage carrier."

"Can you translate what you just said into English, please?"

Chase rolled his eyes.

"Normally, the person who is Awakened, in this case, your father, would start to prepare the next generation, you and your sister, as early as six years old. He would have taught you the abilities particular to your family's lineage, educated you on the history of the War, and shown you how to fight. This is how it is supposed to work. However, your father wanted you to have a childhood and thought he was invincible. That's why we are in the situation we are in. Can you please keep looking for your name?"

I continued to flip through the Es and Fs.

"What do the numbers listed beside each name mean?"

Chase sighed loudly.

"It's the order of magnitude of the individual."

I glanced over my shoulder. If looks could kill, I would have most certainly been dead.

"Meaning?"

"Meaning, the higher the number, the more rare and powerful the human, with nine being the highest."

I turned the page and finally reached the letter G. My finger slid down the names Gomez, Gorscecksky, Gozinsky, Granger, Grastenmeyer, and finally, Grayson. My finger stopped. Grayson, E.W. - eighth order, with a line scratched through it.

I turned to Chase.

"Why does my father's name have a line through it?" I asked, already knowing the answer.

"When a name is crossed out, it means the person is dead," he said, avoiding my gaze.

I could sense he was holding something back.

"What aren't you telling me, Chase?"

"Your father didn't die from complications due to surgery, Amykah. He was assassinated. The Dark bided their time waiting until he was vulnerable, then they killed him."

My breath caught. I doubled over. The thought my dad had been murdered sent a pain ripping through my chest.

"He was killed?" My words were barely a whisper.

Chase wrapped his arm around my shoulder and knelt next to me.

"Amykah, I am so sorry. I didn't want to be the one to tell you. Your father was of the eighth order and a massive threat to the Dark One. He was single-handedly destroying Dark Institutions all across the World. He was a fantastic man and, just like you, a force to be reckoned with."

To hear Chase speak of the impact my father had made eased the pain of his loss a little. He tilted my face up, and our eyes met. A wave of calm flooded through me, washing away the pain. My tears stopped flowing, and my breath returned to normal. He stood with his eyes locked on mine. Brushing a stray hair away from my face, he placed his fingers on my temple as he spoke.

"Amykah, let the memory of your father's death fade. Remember why we are here. You must find your name in the Book and discover the truth of who you are. Can you do that?" he said while his voice erased the pain of my father's death.

I nodded slowly.

My mind felt hazy. I returned to the Book and found my name. It was glowing. Not far below my name was another name I recognized.

"My sister's name is here, but it's not glowing. How is that possible?"

"She has not awakened yet. Sometimes, if there are two or more siblings in the family, the one of the highest order will awaken first, followed by the others. Amykah, please look at your name. What does it say?"

I read out loud, "Grayson, Amykah - ninth order, but that is the highest order there is..." my voice trailed off. I couldn't believe my eyes. I shook my head and then looked at Chase.

"I'm not surprised," he said with that obnoxious, endearing smirk.

I continued, "Knower. Slayer. Healer. Maker. A Master of Qi through which all can be done. This human is incredibly dangerous, not only to the Dark One, but also to..."

"To who?" Chase pressed.

"I don't know."

I watched as, one by one, the words disappeared from the book until the entire page was blank. I searched through the other pages.

"It's blank," I said.

Chase closed the distance between us, trying to look over my shoulder.

"What do you mean it's blank?"

"See," I said, pointing to the Book.

Then, all of a sudden, a letter appeared on the page. I read it out loud.

**I**

More letters appeared as the dark red liquid they were written in bled onto the page. I continued.

**SEE YOU**

Chase's hand gripped my arm as the last two words took form.

**AMYKAH**

**GRAYSON**

I slammed the Book shut, backing right into Chase. My heartbeat thundered in my ears.

"What the hell was that?" I said, feeling the world around me become less solid.

"He knows we are here. He could send someone. We have to go, right now," he said, his voice low and desperate.

Chase grabbed my hand and pulled me toward the door. His grip was so tight I lost feeling in all my fingers. He put his palm on the door, and it dissolved into whirling sand. We stepped through into the dark concrete hallway. My legs gave way while the world continued to whirl around me. Chase pulled me to his chest to keep me from falling.

"Amykah, are you okay?"

Looking up at him through my lashes, I could barely keep my senses.

"Just a bit woozy," I said, minimizing how I was really feeling.

He didn't move. There was barely a breath between us. My skin tingled with him so close.

"Do you believe me now?" he said, searching my eyes for an answer.

"I'm not sure what to believe anymore," I said breathlessly.

My knees felt like they could buckle again at any minute, but I didn't think being this close to Chase would help the situation. I stepped out of his embrace and backed up against the wall. We exchanged glances, and I saw a fire blazing in his eyes.

"Now that you know the truth about who you are, it's time to go save your friends."

"How do you propose we do that? I know I'm of the ninth order and all, but I have no idea what that even means or how to access any of my supposed abilities."

"Simple, I'll keep them all busy while you grab your friends and get the hell out of here," he said with a smile.

"How am I supposed to do that? What if they're hurt or injured? There are too many of those things for you to take on by yourself. What about the other people? We can't just leave them. And what about..."

He gently touched his finger to my mouth.

"Don't worry about me. I can handle myself. You get your friends and get out of here. Do you understand?"

I nodded with his finger still pressed against my lips.

"Let's go," he said.

He took my hand in his. We ran back up the dark, long, twisted hallway, and a sense of knowing that Lexi, Tori, and I would be all right rushed through my body. A vision of us escaping from the Lab through the door to the Warehouse appeared in my mind's eye. Then, I concentrated on Chase in a vain attempt to glimpse his fate through what I could only assume was one of my abilities starting to surface. The vision began to form, and I saw him standing on top of a table. Suddenly, a thick grey fog enveloped the picture in my head, obscuring Chase completely.

Tossing me a look of disapproval, he said, "Whatever you're doing, stop it."

"I wasn't doing anything," I said, feigning ignorance but weakened by the attempt of using my newly discovered ability.

He didn't break his stride. "Yes, you were, and it won't work on me," he said with finality.

Chase obviously could tell I was trying to glimpse his fate. He must have shut me out with his ability to shield. But why wouldn't he want me to see if he was going to be alright? My mind offered me an answer I didn't particularly like. The only reason he wouldn't want me to see his future was if he had something to hide.

As we rounded the final corner, the light from the Lab poured in, driving the darkness away. At the edge, where light met dark, we stood hidden in the shadows. Watching him assess the threats ahead of us, I wondered what else he might be hiding from me.

# CHAPTER 15

"**I**'LL GO FIRST AND create a distraction. You get Tori & Lexi," Chase said.

"That's it? *That's* your big plan? How exactly am I going to do that? Last we knew, Lexi was lying on a table surrounded by things in white coats, and Tori was locked in a glass cage."

"Like I said, I will create a distraction that will hopefully keep everything busy with me, and they won't even notice you."

"Hopefully?" I said, my voice raising an octave.

"You'll be fine. You got this," he said with a smile. "I will keep them away from you for as long as I possibly can. Here..." he reached into his boot, pulled out a dagger, and handed it to me.

It looked so foreign in my hands. I had never used a weapon of any kind before. I turned it over, feeling the leather handle and seeing my reflection in its metal. I felt Chase watching me.

"Use the pointy end. It's more effective that way," he said with a snicker. Then, his eyes darkened while his smile faded away. "I need you to do something for me, Amykah. I need you to promise that whatever you see, hear, or think may be happening to me, you *must* keep going no matter what. Do you understand?"

"But," I started to protest.

He clasped his hand on my shoulder, bringing his face inches from mine.

Any questions or concerns I had vanished under his touch. My mind was a blank slate, ready for whatever Chase was going to say.

"You will only focus on saving Lexi and Tori. You must keep going no matter what happens to me. Now, wait here until you hear the signal."

I blinked rapidly, trying to remember what I had wanted to say, when I realized Chase had started walking away from me.

"Wait, what's the signal?"

"Oh, you will know," he said with a mischievous grin.

Before disappearing into the light, Chase stopped and gave me a wink.

Within minutes, an ear-splitting alarm went off. That must be the signal. I shoved the dagger into my boot and rushed into the light. The crashing of metal, combined with breaking glass, growls, and blood-curdling screams, assailed my ears. I wanted to stop and see the hellfire Chase must have been bringing down, but I was compelled to find Tori.

I found her standing in a glass cage, with a faint smile on her lips, staring at what I could only assume was the carnage behind me. Tori didn't even look at me when I approached. I reached for the door handle, but there wasn't one. No latch either. Finally, she saw me.

Her eyes widened as she pounded on the glass. Tori's mouth was moving, but I could only hear the screams and crashes from the fight behind me. I shrugged, shaking my head and motioning to my predicament.

How am I going to get her out of here? I put my hand on the cool glass. The thought of our freedom slipped away with every minute. This can't be the end. The instant the thought entered my mind, a heat emanated from my hand. The familiar thrumming sensation I felt outside the General's office returned. My vision blurred slightly, and the glass transformed into sand under my touch.

Tori leapt away as I pulled my hand off the glass and examined it. I didn't have time to question what was happening. A solution presented itself, and I needed to take it. I pressed my hand against the glass. It quickly started to change form and fall away like sand. The glimmering white dust swirled around me, creating a portal. I stepped through it and into the cage with Tori.

"What the actual fuck, Amykah?" Tori said, backing herself up against the opposite side of the cage.

"I'll explain everything later. This is the only way out. We need to get Lexi and get out of here," I said, reaching my hand toward her.

Tori grabbed my hand. When we reached the other side of the glass wall, she shook her head and swayed a bit. I grabbed her by the shoulders to steady her. She shook me off.

"I'm fine. Let's get out of here," she growled.

"First, we have to get Lexi, and I need your help."

I raced over to Lexi with Tori right behind me. She was unconscious on the table. There were no more tubes attached to her arm, but there was a pulsating red scar on her abdomen. I pulled her shirt down to cover the wound, unsure of what was to come from whatever they had done to her.

"Lexi, wake up," I whispered.

I shook her by the shoulders and leaned down next to her ear.

"Lexi, I need you to wake up now."

"You better hurry," Tori said, eyeing the commotion behind us.

Lexi stirred and fluttered her eyes while she let out a small moan.

"Tori, help me sit her up."

In one swift motion, Tori had Lexi on her feet with an arm wrapped around her waist. I flanked Lexi on the other side, lending my support.

"Tori and I will hold you up, but you must move your feet, Lex," I said.

"Mmmm, hmmm," she responded, eyes still closed and head hanging down.

We made our way toward the door, with Tori virtually dragging Lexi behind us. I glanced over my shoulder to see Chase standing on top of a table, just like I had seen in my vision, but this time, he was covered in black sludge and swinging his machete at the closest thing, sending its head flying.

We moved as quickly as we could. Lexi slowly came back to her senses while passing by other captives pounding on the glass, pleading for help.

"But what about the others?" Tori asked motioning with her head to the glass cages.

"We don't have time to help the others. Chase will do his best. Right now, we have to get out of here," I said, hating myself for leaving them behind.

I would have sworn out of the corner of my eye, the edge of Tori's mouth barely curled up into a smile, and then it was gone.

Even though Lexi had gained more control of her body, we still couldn't move fast enough. Her toe caught on the floor, and she tripped. This caused a domino effect. I slammed into the table, which sent the metal chains that hung from the frame clanging together. Within a split second, Tori spun us around and kicked free one of the metal posts holding up the frame. She turned it over, ready for what was to come.

The noise from our minor calamity turned the head of a creature similar to the one I saw outside Club Inferno. Its scraggly black hair shone in the fluorescent lights with its scissor-like teeth gleaming. It was smiling, if you could call it that, as its black, vacuous eyes focused on me. It made a high-pitched trilling noise and was shortly accompanied by another of its kind. Now, there were two of them. They took off at a sprint with their scorpion tails whipping wildly back and forth.

Tori swung the metal post just when one of the creatures leapt in the air and sent it careening in the opposite direction. I reflexively reached for the dagger in my boot and threw it at the demoness creature coming at me. A howl reverberated through the room as it slid to a stop at my feet with the dagger stuck between its dead eyes.

The commotion caught the attention of whatever Chase hadn't killed yet. All eyes turned toward us. The remaining creatures and humans alike bared down on us, trampling over the bodies of the dead littering the floor. It was now or never.

"Run!" I yelled.

Lexi and Tori sprinted toward the door. I was close on their heels.

We were almost there, only a few more feet, and we'd escape. Lexi's feet got tangled, dropping her to her knees. Tori picked her up off the ground and ran to the door.

I made the mistake of looking back. All I could see were fangs, fur, scales, and eyes coming after us. One creature launched toward me, thin filamentous tentacles whipping around its face. I closed my eyes, waiting for the inevitable, but when it didn't come, I opened them to find Chase by my side with his machete in hand, covered in fresh black frothing ooze. Its head was next to me, with tentacles still flailing. Before I even knew what had happened, one of the tentacles wound itself around my ankle, and a searing hot pain shot through my leg. Chase quickly ripped the tentacle off my leg and punted the head away from us. He lifted me to my feet.

My leg burned to the bone, not allowing me to put my total weight through it. Tori and Lexi were already holding the door open. I looked at Chase, not knowing if I would ever see him again. He must have read the concern on my face.

"I'll be fine. Now go, and whatever you do, don't look back."

He turned his back toward me, taking a wide stance, machete at the ready.

"Come on, Amykah. We need to go now," Tori said, pushing Lexi through the door. I limped toward the doorway to our world. Tori came and wrapped her arm around my waist, carrying me through into the warehouse. The door crashed shut behind us, metal crunching on metal, sealing Chase's fate. I just stood there staring at the door.

Seeing my hesitation, Tori barked, "We need to keep moving in case he's not able to hold them off."

The dim red glow from the exit sign lit the way from across the warehouse. It was still dark outside, with the occasional splinter of light shining down from the windows above.

We made our way through the dark, Lexi leaning on Tori for support and me limping. Halfway to the exit, crunching metal stopped us in our tracks. We all turned to see who had come through the door and what our fate beheld. There was nothing. Then, what was left of Lexi's color drained from her face.

"What the..." she said, pointing to where the door was disappearing right in front of our eyes, leaving only a solid concrete wall behind.

I squinted, trying to see any shadows or movement, but there was nothing.

"Come on, the door doesn't matter. We are almost out of here. Keep moving," Tori snapped.

We all set our feet moving forward, our freedom from this night of hell just twenty feet ahead. Lexi stopped.

In between coughs, she asked, "Do you feel that?"

Tori and I exchanged glances, knowing what was to come.

"We need to move right now," I said, panic swelling within my chest.

Wide-eyed and pale, Lexi went to run but fell to her knees in a coughing fit. Tori and I quickly pulled Lexi to her feet. My lungs were struggling for air, but it didn't matter. The searing pain in my leg kept me focused.

"Tori, do whatever you must, but get to the door. I'll help Lexi."

"Amykah, what is happening? Are we going to die?" Lexi asked between gasps. I watched as her eyes rolled to the back of her head. She fell to the floor, and I went down with her.

I looked up to see Tori on her hands and knees, crawling toward the door, then suddenly dropping to the floor near the exit. She lay there gasping as terror filled her eyes. I opened my mouth in a vain attempt to breath, but nothing came. My vision was fading fast. Tori and Lexi were not moving. I made one last attempt to get up, but gravity slammed me back to the ground, almost cracking my skull on the hard concrete.

I rolled onto my back. Short little gasps were all I could manage as my chest rose and fell rapidly. The red exit light taunted me from above, just a few short feet away. I turned my head to the side. My vision slowly tunneled with darkness threatening to eclipse everything when a pair of black boots splattered with what I thought looked like spots of brown paint came into view. Maybe we were going to be okay. I slowly gazed up at the shadowy figure standing over me. My eyes refused to focus while my lids threatened to close for good. Those shoes, why did those shoes look so familiar?

# CHAPTER 16

MY EYES FLEW OPEN. I reflexively gasped and air filled my lungs. Light forced its way through the blinds, highlighting a nightstand with an empty overturned bottle of vodka. I was in my own bedroom. A sigh of relief escaped my lips.

I tried to remember what had happened last night at the club, but couldn't. The more I concentrated, the more elusive the memories became. I pushed off the covers and discovered a deep ache permeating every part of my body. As I sat up, waves of dizziness washed over me. It must have been one hell of a night. I can't remember how I made it to bed, let alone why I would be wearing my boots. Maybe splashing some water on my face would help. I stood and shuffled my way to the bathroom.

The cold water was refreshing, helping to wash away the fogginess in my head. I leaned over, took a drink, and let the water soothe my parched throat.

"Remember," a voice murmured.

I spun around half expecting to be greeted by someone behind me, but instead, found myself facing an empty room. I chalked it up to likely still being drunk after whatever we did last night.

"Remember," the voice said, this time louder and with more urgency.

It sounded like he was standing right next to me. I gripped the countertop as my world began to spin. Closing my eyes, the veil between me and what happened last night was torn to shreds. Every detail came flooding back in an instant. Going to the club. Lexi missing. Breaking into the warehouse with Tori. Having my mind hacked by a Karekidin. Being rescued by Chase. Lexi on a table. Tori in a glass cage. A Book of the Dark. My father's murder. My importance in it all. Having abilities. Killing a half-human, half-demon creature with a dagger. Leaving Chase behind with the door slamming shut. Black boots with brown spots. Then nothing.

My head pounded. I gingerly opened my eyes. Somehow, I had ended up on the bathroom floor staring at the ceiling. I could only assume the flood of information had overwhelmed my nervous system, causing me to pass out.

A loud thud outside my bedroom startled me back to reality. I scrambled to my feet, nearly knocking my head on the bathroom counter. My muscles tensed as I grabbed my trusty baseball bat and headed toward the bedroom door. Peering through the tiny crack, I saw Lexi sitting beside the couch on the floor, rubbing her face. Tori was sprawled out in the chair, mouth open, snoring.

"Ow, that hurt," Lexi said to no one in particular.

Leaving my bat leaning against the wall, I rushed over to her.

"Oh my gosh, you're okay," I said, throwing my arms around her.

"Umm, no. Hitting the floor with my face hurts. Myks, what's with the bat?"

"I wasn't sure who or what was out here, and I wanted to protect myself, especially after last night," I said looking her up and down. "When did you change back into your clothes?"

I lifted her shirt to see the pulsing red scar that wasn't there.

She pushed my hand away, pulling down her shirt.

"What on earth are you talking about, Amykah? These are the same clothes I have been wearing all night," she said, raising an eyebrow while making her way back onto the couch.

I sat beside her. "Ugh, I don't. I just wanted to make sure you were okay."

"Why wouldn't I be okay? I just fell off the couch. Nothing I haven't done before," she said, laughing and groaning simultaneously.

Tori stirred in the chair, licked her lips, and closed her mouth. There were no bruises, cuts, or scrapes, and all her clothes were completely intact.

"Yeah, last night certainly *was* crazy," she said slowly, eyes still closed.

Holding her head in her hands, Lexi grunted, "We've *never* had a night like that before and hopefully won't have another one for a very long time,"

"How can you guys be so calm? We almost died last night," I said.

Tori's eyes flung open as she whipped herself into a sitting position.

"So, we had a lot of drinks, and I mean a lot, but no one was going to die. You don't have to be so dramatic about it all," Tori said, rolling her eyes. "Are you still drunk? Because I think I might be."

She returned to her previous position and closed her eyes.

I jumped up and started pacing, albeit with a limp.

"No, I'm not still drunk. I'm not sure I ever was drunk."

I shifted my gaze to Lexi and plopped back onto the couch beside her, resting my throbbing leg.

"Lex, what do you remember?"

She wiped away some drool from her mouth and rubbed her forehead.

"Well, I remember being at the club, you and Tori hanging at the bar while I was on the dance floor. I saw you dash out of the room, and the rest is a bit of a blur."

"Tori, what about you?" I asked, throwing a pillow in her general direction.

"Ugh, I went wandering around, and then you found me. You were freaking out because you couldn't find Lexi. We split up and went looking for her…"

I interrupted her.

"So, it *was* real."

Lexi looked at me as if I had three heads.

"Why wouldn't it be real?"

"Well, with all the people being held captive, the creatures, the experiments," I said.

Tori snickered.

"I'm pretty sure all those people being held captive wanted it that way, especially the ones in cages."

"How can you say that? *You* were being held in a cage against your will," I said. Then I turned toward Lexi, pointing my finger at her, "and *you* were on an operating table with a tube in your arm and a creature doing who knows what to you. We barely escaped the Lab and left Chase to fight them off. Then, while trying to escape the warehouse, we were suffocated until we passed out. Which begs the question, how did we all end up here if we were passed out on the warehouse floor?"

I looked at Lexi and then at Tori. Their eyes were wide, mouths agape. They were looking at me as if I had lost my mind. No one spoke. They just stared. I know I wasn't making the whole thing up. Well, at least, I'm pretty sure.

"Wow, Amykah, it sounds like everything you drank really went to your head," Tori said, shaking her head.

"Look, I know I must sound crazy, but it all seemed very real," I said.

"Don't you think we would know if we were held captive in some laboratory and had been experimented on? Where are the cuts and bruises? The surgical incisions? How do our clothes not have holes, tears, and dirt on them if we were fighting for our lives?" Tori challenged.

She made some very valid points contradicting what I remembered.

"Then how did we get home?" I probed.

"Well, three really gorgeous guys were buying us drinks all night. You were even making out with some hot guy, which is so unlike you, Myks. He was tall, with blonde spiky hair and a painted-on grey shirt emphasizing every ripple on his muscular body. I was so proud of you," Lexi said with a wink. "Even though they tried to get us to go with them, I think we caught an Uber home instead. But the details are a bit fuzzy for me. Then we woke up here, to you and your bat."

"Did he have grey eyes? The guy I was making out with?" I asked, heart pounding to think maybe Chase was real.

"I didn't get a clear look. I was kind of busy myself," Lexi said with a sly grin.

"He had blue eyes," Tori interjected.

My shoulders slumped at her response.

Lexi's eyebrows furrowed while she fidgeted with her hands. "Hey Myks, weren't you telling me earlier you had been to see your *doctor*," Lexi said, clearly not wanting to say anything about the kind of doctor I had been to in front of Tori.

"Um, yes, but what does that have to do with anything?"

"Do you think it's possible your new *vitamins,* combined with everything we drank last night, could have caused you to have a vivid dream?" Lexi asked, avoiding eye contact with me.

"How could vitamins and alcohol give you crazy life-like dreams?" Tori snickered.

I knew what Lexi was trying to insinuate, and I had to admit it could have been possible. The hallucinations started yesterday morning and had continued throughout the day. No one else saw them. Not at the bus stop, on the street, at the doctor's office, or at the club. I couldn't even find the supposed letter and book my dad had left me, let alone the box it had been sent in with the note from the lawyer. Had I created this whole story in my head? I remembered Tori and I searching for Lexi and seeing Chase, well, who I thought was Chase. Had all the repressed emotions from the past year created another psychotic break?

"Um, I think you're right, Lexi. I need to go lie down for a bit. My head is throbbing," I said, retreating to my bedroom. Just as I closed my door, a tear trickled down my face. I grabbed my phone off the nightstand and sat on my bed. I found what I was looking for, the one contact I had hoped never to call again: Harbor View Psychiatric Hospital.

I can't live like this anymore. It had all felt so real, but it wasn't. I was still that broken girl whose mind could not be trusted and needed to be medicated just to function. My hand shook violently as I went to touch the call button. Suddenly, my phone rang. I fumbled it, catching it just before it hit the floor. I stared at the screen.

Do I really want to answer this call? That was a definite no, but she had been calling me all day. I guess I can't avoid her forever. I answered, and she started in before I could even utter hello.

"Why the hell haven't you been answering my calls? It's just like you to avoid me like you do everything else in your life."

"You know, now is not a good time, Kate," I said, hoping just this once she would listen to me.

"I don't care whether or not it is a good time for you. God, you can be so selfish. You always have been," she paused, "Look Amykah, that's not why I called. Have you heard from Mom?"

"No, not for a couple of days. Why?"

"I can't get a hold of her. I've tried her cell, but it goes straight to voicemail. I tried her office, and her assistant said she had to go out of town on an emergency."

"What emergency?" I said quickly, trying to get a word in.

"How am I supposed to know? I haven't been able to get ahold of her. Her assistant said Mom didn't actually call in, but instead, she sent an email."

"An email? That doesn't sound like her."

Now, I was getting worried.

"Did you try some of her friends?" I asked, but as soon as the words left my mouth, I knew it was a mistake to question my dear sister's actions.

"Of course I did. What do you think, that I'm an idiot? I have been doing everything I could to find out where she is and if she is okay. And what have you been doing? You haven't even bothered to notice our mom has been missing for days."

I stayed silent. Often, that is the best thing to do when dealing with my sister.

"You need to meet me in Chicago. I already bought you a ticket and..."

I raised my voice over hers, something I usually would never do, but I felt this situation warranted it.

"Kate, there is no way I can get on a plane. I had something terrible happen last night. I need to go..."

"I don't care what *you* need. There is *always* something terrible happening to you. Have you ever once stopped to think, let alone ask how I have been this past year? No, not even once, and why should you? You are so wrapped up in yourself you couldn't even see anyone else's pain if you tried." She paused, taking a breath, "Look, something is wrong. I can feel it. So, here's what you are going to do. You will get on the plane, and I will pick you up from the airport first thing in the morning, no excuses, Amykah. You need to put your big girl pants on and help me find out what happened to our mother."

Nothing but silence. She had hung up. Again, it's not surprising, given our history. I threw my phone and dropped my head in my hands. What did she know about what I was going through and how it felt to be unable to trust yourself? Absolutely nothing. I don't even remember her coming to visit me. She was the one who abandoned me first. I honestly had never given my sister a second thought after being committed to the mental institution. I guess she wasn't entirely wrong in her accusations, and I suppose that's what stung the most. There was a soft tap as a tear struck my leather pants.

I stood up, tore off the black skin-tight tank top, and threw it, grabbing the nearest shirt off the floor. Next for the pants. I reached into the back pockets to fish out anything I might have left in them from last night. My only treasure was a crumpled-up piece of paper.

Unfolding it, I read the words slowly, recognizing the scrawled handwriting as my body started shaking. My knees gave way, and I fell to the floor, still clutching the little piece of paper.

*All of it was real.*
*They have your mother.*
*Trust no one. I'll be in touch.*
*~Chase*

A gentle knock came at the door as Lexi stuck her head in.

"Everything alright, Myks?"

I shoved the note into my pocket and wiped my face.

"Yeah, just got done talking with Kate."

Lexi plopped down beside me.

"Well, that explains why you're on the floor in tears."

Her arm around my shoulder felt comforting. I relaxed into her, letting her support me.

"She can't reach my mom, and it's been days." I took a deep breath. "She's booked a plane ticket for me, leaving first thing in the morning."

"Are you going to go?"

"If it were just for Kate, no. But for my mom, yes. I owe her that, at least."

"Ok, then. I will help you pack."

Lexi stood up and offered me her hand.

Taking it, I stood, shaking my head.

"You are most certainly *not* helping me pack. I still have to figure out how to get myself out of these stupid pants…"

She laughed as she patted my ass.

"Alright, I'll pick Tori up off the chair, and we'll go grab some breakfast."

"Lexi, it's noon."

She glanced toward the clock on the nightstand.

"So, it is. Then we will go pick up some lunch and bring it back."

She bounded out of the room, yelling Tori's name.

I carefully took the note out of my pocket and read it again.

*All of it was real.*
*They have your mother.*
*Trust no one. I'll be in touch.*
*~Chase*

My leg started throbbing. I stripped off the leather pants to find a thin red stripe winding around my ankle. I traced its outline with my finger. If this was real, I wonder what else could be real.

I walked over to the wall that separated the bathroom from my bedroom. Heart pounding, I opened and closed my fist, then placed my palm against it. Nothing happened. I shook my hands, took a deep breath, and put my hand on the wall again. When I closed my eyes, I focused all my energy on the desire to get to the other side. A warmth emanated from my palm while my body thrummed to a crescendo. The wall gave way beneath me. My eyes snapped open to see a portal of swirling sand. I pulled my hand away, and it became solid again.

I swayed from my efforts, grabbing onto the doorframe for support. A smile spread across my lips. All of it *had* been real. I still can't explain why Tori and Lexi couldn't remember the events of last night, let alone how they didn't have any injuries to show for it. There has got to be some kind of magic at play. I never thought I'd be saying this, but magic is real, demons are real, and my mother has been taken by the Dark. I read Chase's note one last time and started packing.

BONUS CHAPTER / NEWLETTER SIGN-UP

Do you want to find out what happened to Amykah when she woke up in Harbor View? Get your FREE copy of Awakening: The Lost Chapter at https://BookHip.com/VGZAAJM

# ABOUT THE AUTHOR

 A.G. Hughes writes fast-paced young adult urban fantasy novellas full of magic, adventure and betrayal with unexpected twists and turns that will keep you guessing. There is always something deeper lurking in her writing, but fair warning, it may lead you down a path of questioning everything you know to be real...if you let it.

She loves her family, being a mom, reinventing herself on a regular basis, and being a scribe for the stories that want to be told.

You can often find A.G. Hughes in Texas, where she currently lives. If she isn't there, she is likely traveling by plane, train, car, or RV to exciting places looking for an adventure.